MONSTERS
AND THE
SUPERNATURAL

MONSTERS
AND THE
SUPERNATURAL

A YOUNG PERSON'S GUIDE

Author
J.J.MOORE

Illustrator
K.B.MOON

NEW
HOLLAND

Contents

INTRODUCTION

Many years ago I lived in a house in the middle of Melbourne. It had been built in the 1940s by a digger who had just returned from Papua New Guinea where he had been fighting the Japanese. He and his wife lived there all of their married lives. His lovely wife had a heart attack on the front lawn and the old soldier died in the house too.

Soon after, my young family and I moved into the nice old house. When you are older you will realise that not all business people tell the truth – we certainly weren't told what had happened in the house just a couple of months before.

It wasn't a problem, though, because the old man (let's call him Victor) made sure we were safe. Sometimes when I went to the shops to buy nappies, Victor would come up to the front door, open the lock and walk down the corridor to check on things before walking out again.

Once we were watching TV and footsteps came down the corridor to the lounge room door. We both looked up but nobody was there. I got up and checked the kids, but they were fast asleep.

I don't know if any of you have lived out in the country. I once lived in a little town where less than 200 years ago Aboriginal Australians roamed the land. At night it was possible to feel the tribes walking among the gum trees, whispering to each other as they flitted through the night, even though they were long gone.

The first settlers in Australia heard reports of a creature called the Bunyip. The Aboriginals were terrified of this animal. It lived in waterways and ate up little children, just like your younger brothers and sisters, if they got too close to the water. You might sometimes rather dislike your siblings and wish that horrible things happened to them, but you would not want a bunyip to get them. They would be drawn down to the bottom of a billabong by the bunyip's terrifying claws and hungry snout. At night the bunyip sang for its relatives, a deep 'whoop whoop'.

The English scoffed at this story and thought the Aboriginals must be pretty darn silly to believe in such a far-fetched tale.

Are ghosts shy? Do they even know we exist?

The Aboriginals got the last laugh though. Archaeologists have found that there *was* a giant marsupial that most likely lived in wetlands. It was bigger than a horse and had large claws almost nine inches long, as well as a proboscis for a nose, just like an elephant's only shorter. The bunyip really existed in Australia but perhaps died out just before Europeans arrived.

It may still survive in remote pockets of the vast Australian continent, just like hundreds of other 'mythical' creatures.

This book will take you on a journey into remote corners of the globe and deep into man's belief in the supernatural. We'll look at different monsters and spirits, ghouls and critters, back through the ages. They can't be inventions, because our imaginations aren't that rich.

None of this book is fiction, it is all fact … maybe.

Who knows what horrors are lurking in the bush?

CHAPTER 1

TAKEN FOR A TERROR RIDE

Imagine that you wake up in the middle of the night. Rather than waking up warm and toasty and filled with cheerful thoughts, you feel an unexplainable terror. The terror is overwhelming. You try and sit up but two clawed hands press down on your chest, pinning you to the mattress like a piece of flattened road kill.

Your whole body is paralysed with fear. What's worse is that it's getting more and more difficult to breathe. Those ghostly hands seem to be tearing into your flesh at the same time as your breath rattles out of your compressed lungs!

You are being ridden by a 'night mare' or a 'night hag'.

Gradually you force your eyes open. Just discernible in the gloom is a hooked-nosed, green-eyed old biddy glaring at you and pouring hate into your soul.

Then your bedroom door opens, the light switch is thrown and there is your mother. All of a sudden you can spring up and breathe easy; the 'night hag' is banished.

This kind of story is very common and lots of people describe the same terrifying feeling. But in fact it might be that they have just experienced a medical complaint called 'sleep paralysis'. Sleep paralysis is often caused when people are very tired and run down. Their natural sleeping process is disturbed.

In a normal night's sleep you will gradually descend into unconsciousness and leave the world behind. The body becomes relaxed and cools down while it repairs and restores your cells. But two or three times a night you will enter REM sleep (you can tell if somebody is in REM because their eyelids flutter). This is the dreaming stage of sleep. Now of course while dreaming people imagine they are running, fighting, talking, flying and doing all sorts of physical activity. If you let your body do these things you would thrash around in bed and probably hurt yourself. So as you enter REM sleep your brain is disengaged from the rest of your body so that it cannot move your limbs and you lie still, no matter what you are dreaming.

'I didn't mean to wake you – Have you seen me false teef?'

Some scientists think that sleep paralysis occurs when the body is still in REM stage but the brain is not. That would account for the paralysed body – but not the feeling of terror.

The stories of those who have encountered night hags around the world are remarkably similar. There are often strange smells and even the sounds of approaching footsteps. Often only red eyes are visible. Once the person wakes up a great weight is lifted off the chest, followed by an almost unbelievable sense of relief. It happens to both men and women and somewhere between 15 and 50% of the population have had the experience. It can even happen in daylight while people are just having a little nap and don't get close to entering REM sleep, which often occurs only after 90 minutes of sleep.

All say they sit up and look around immediately after they are free.

But that is only what happens to those who survive. What are the experiences of those who die? Many people still die in their sleep – are they carried off by the night hag?

'NIGHT MARES' AROUND THE WORLD

These stories have been told for thousands of years and are reported all around the world. They are all remarkably similar: the 'night mare' is a spirit woman who is damned for some awful crime.

In Scandinavia the 'mare' is an evil damned woman who is still alive. In the dead of night her soul floats beyond her body and fastens upon some poor individual who is sleeping nearby. Americans have a similar superstition, but they believe that witches ride at night and seek out poor victims to 'ride'. The Chinese believe that it is a ghost and they actually have a phrase that means 'ghost pushing down on the bed'. Remarkably even the Mongols, who are nomadic folk, experience a similar phenomenon which they call 'dark press'. Throughout Asia and including countries such as Thailand, Cambodia, Vietnam, Malaysia, India and Pakistan, countless millions of people refer to the condition as 'pressing' or the 'ghost push'.

No one wants to be ridden by the night hag.

The Pashtun culture in Afghanistan and Pakistan have a particularly scary form. They believe in the khapasa. The khapasa is a ghost without thumbs. It sits on its victim's chest and tries to strangle them, but since it does not have an opposable thumb it has to push down on the chest as well. The khapasa makes a mewling sound as it rocks back and forth on its victim's chest, desperately trying to stop them breathing.

In mountainous Nepal the khyaak, as it is known, hides under a house's staircase during the day. The khyaak is the spirit of a woman who died during childbirth and she emerges from her shadowy hidey-hole at night-time to sit on the chests of young children.

Europe has hundreds of night hags. Hungary believes that wraiths, witches, fairies and demon lovers can all be responsible for disturbing dreams. In Malta they believe that to rid your household of the female Haddiela you should sleep with a silver spoon under your pillow. The Latvians are attacked by a Lietuvēns. This is the soul of a woman who had been hanged or drowned, and to ward off her attack you must move the little toe of your left foot. This shows how bad the paralysis can be – it takes a massive effort to move even the smallest limb of the body.

While some sceptics might poo-poo the whole idea of night hags, I think they would find it difficult to explain how these stories from all around the world are almost exactly the same?

FASCINATING FACTS
THE SHADOWMAN
· ·

Maybe the scariest part of waking from a terrified slumber is the appearance of what thousands of people have reported as a 'shadowman'. Commonly these figures stand at the foot of the bed, just beyond direct sight. At other times they are glanced as they disappear into a cupboard, go out the bedroom door or even slip behind the curtains.

Most worrying are the 'dark masses', as these phenomena are also known, which just hang about, flickering in the peripheral vision. They refuse to appear and refuse to disappear.

'He wet his bed and all!'
– International night hags swap notes.

FASCINATING FACTS
INCUBUS AND SUCCUBUS
· ·

These two terrifying creatures are like the night hag, but instead of pressing down on a sleeper's chest, the incubus and succubus sleep with their victims. In doing this they drain the life force out of their prey, making them waste away to nothing.

I'm not really sure they exist. Superstitious people in the past may have invented them so that they could explain why some people got weaker and weaker as diseases such as cancer took their toll.

CHAPTER 2

GHOSTS IN HISTORY

You might have a friend who poo-poos the whole idea of ghosts.

'I've never seen one so of course they don't exist!' is the common refrain. Well I tell you something, I've never seen an African tiger fish, but does that mean *they* don't exist?

I've never seen a black hole out in space pulling everything into it that strays within one light year's distance away. Apparently there are millions and billions of them out in the universe. In fact, scientists reckon that invisible dark matter is four times more common in our universe than plain old matter (stuff) that we can see. And do you think they have actually seen or recorded this dark matter? No! They have just used mathematics to work out that it must exist.

I'm sure those sceptical friends of yours will believe whatever a couple of boffins in lab coats say is true straight away. But they will ignore what thousands and thousands of other people say has happened to them.

That they have seen a ghost.

Now, there are two kinds of people who believe in ghosts. There are those that have never really believed in them until a strange experience has forced them to rethink their ideas. That's the kind of ghostly experience you'll hear about in this book. It's quite amazing how many people say 'I never believed in ghosts until …'

The other kind of person who believes in ghosts are mediums. I reckon mediums (most at least) are big rip-off merchants. They walk into a house and say ridiculous things like 'Oooh, I can feel the presence of seven dead people here. Upstairs there is a little girl who is looking for her poodle called Ruffles. In the corner there is an old man who is still angry at his wife because she took his winning lottery card and ran off to Hawaii with the gardener. Oh and living under the stairs is a little old lady wearing purple knickers …' and so on and so on. They are the people who like to make money out of ghosts and will basically tell you anything you want to hear.

What they don't tell you is that people have believed in ghosts for tens of thousands and perhaps hundreds of thousands of years.

Ghosts need clean knickers too!

FASCINATING FACTS
CHINESE SUPERSTITION AND EUNUCHS
· · · · · · · · · · · · · · · · · ·

For thousands of years the Chinese have believed that to get to a happy afterlife your whole body has to buried in one piece. This made it very difficult for eunuchs.

A eunuch is a person who has had his testicles removed either as a punishment or so he could become an attendant to the Chinese Emperor! Most were given this surgery when they were young. Their testicles and penis were then placed in a little jar and the eunuch had to carry them around with him until he died. They would then be placed in his coffin with his corpse before being buried.

But of course some eunuchs lost their little 'package'. So of course they had to steal some other poor fellow's bits and carry *them* to the grave. Obviously it didn't matter that it was *your* whole body that was buried as long as it had all the requisite parts!

Chinese people are pretty concerned with this, as if you don't enter the happy afterlife with a proper burial you come back as a ghost. And there are no happy Chinese ghosts it seems. They are all miserable and angry and always try to take out this anger on the living.

There are some things you DEFINITELY don't want to lose.

Many cultures throughout history have buried their dead in graves filled with weapons, food, clothes and cups. Even our cousins the Neanderthals covered their loved ones with flowers and buried them deep under the floor of their caves to make sure they were comfortable as they turned to dust.

Why?

Usually to make sure that the dead were happy in the afterlife and did not come back to haunt the ones they left behind. Lots of civilisations, including the Ancient Greeks and Ancient Chinese, believed that they had to provide food for their ancestors long after burial or else the dead ancestors would come back to cause trouble and bad luck.

Many ghostly tales are told by the Ancients. Pliny the Younger in Ancient Rome was the first to describe a ghost as a bearded old man who would float around and rattle his chains.

The figure was clothed in rags, horribly emaciated and covered in thick matted hair that went down almost to his knees. The ghost's appearances were so common that the splendid house it inhabited was abandoned. Fortunately, a philosopher called Athenodorus heard of the disturbance and decided to mount a ghostly stake-out. When he heard the rattling chains he confronted the ghostly old man, who promptly disappeared. Athenodorus marked the spot where he had last seen the ghost. The next morning, they dug up the floor and found the skeleton of a man bound in chains. The bones were relocated and given a lovely burial ceremony. The spirit was seen no more. So this ancient tale could also be the first story of an exorcism.

In fact many ghosts that are observed today are almost exactly like those from the past.

Many think ghosts are trapped in this dimension.

APPARITIONS

These are figures which usually follow a set pattern, almost as if they are a tape recording. One of the scariest I have heard of was a grey woman who would burst into one bedroom at any hour of the day (or night) and soundlessly mutter to herself as she desperately searched for a person or thing. She opened draws or cupboards and even peered behind the curtains. She never looked at the terrified resident and totally ignored them. She would then silently storm out of the room without finding what she was looking for.

Another common feature of apparitions is that they are not aware of any renovations that may have been made to their house. In a small rectory in Western Victoria, the residents would often see a scullery maid carrying tea for her mistress up the stairs to the second storey. The only problem was the stairs had been relocated years before – so the poor soul floated up in empty air, showing everyone her ghostly knickers! (I think they might have been called bloomers in those days.)

Many ghostly monk processions have been sighted in the dead of night. It's pretty scary, especially when their legs appear to be chopped off because the floor has been raised.

Ghostly knicker alert!

Some of these imprint ghosts go about their business without ever being seen or showing their faces. Spooky examples of this are when footsteps walk up a path and knock loudly but nobody is there, a lounge door slams closed at the same time every day, or a phone rings but nobody is on the line.

While apparitions can be pretty terrifying when seen the first few times, they never try to scare people because they are just 'doing their thing'. Another way to describe these experiences is 'residual hauntings' – something left over or imprinted from another time.

TIME SLIPS

These are in some ways similar to apparitions, but instead of one figure appearing it is almost as if the witness is placed back in time. Many a visitor to an ancient battlefield has been astounded to hear the sounds of swords clashing against armour, people screaming as their limbs are lopped off, or maybe just the sound of thousands of marching feet. At other times visitors to stately manor houses have found themselves surrounded by people in costumes dating back hundreds of years. It's kind of like when you visit Nanna's house and she asks what that strange, buzzing contraption in your hand is, while you look at the boiled lollies and dried out old herbs and pickles that have been there for years.

THE OUIJA BOARD
· ·

When you first heard about Ouija boards you might have thought that they are sacred items used for hundreds of years by wise gypsy women. Perhaps they are treasured items that had been handed down through the generations as the gypsy caravans travelled through the mountains and forests of Europe.

Wrong! They were invented by an American who wanted to make a lot of cash, about one hundred years ago! In 1890 Charles Kennard and some associates produced a new 'talking board' for when people sought to get in touch with spirits. It was easy to use, with letters and numbers as well as 'Yes' and 'No' written in the corners. It came supplied with a movable pointer (planchette), so that people could move it around and spell out messages. Kennard asked the board what it wanted to be called and it spelled out O-U-I-J-A and then helpfully provided a translation: it meant 'good luck'.

It did mean good luck – for the manufacturers! They made lots of money before selling the rights to Hasbro games. Hasbro still sells them and you can even get one in your favourite colour.

Of course, you can make your own with a bit of cardboard, a texta, a glass and some gullible friends!

MALEVOLENT SPIRITS

Unlike apparitions, malevolent spirits do interact with mortal folk. If a malevolent spirit sees you it will have one goal: to scare the bejesuspoop out of you!

One of the creepiest malevolent spirits I have ever investigated lived in a perfectly harmless looking suburban house in a perfectly ordinary looking street. The specialty of this spirit was to place her nasty green face right in front of the faces of sleeping children before waking them up by gently stroking their cheeks. The children woke to find her blazing red eyes centimetres away, while her pointed fingernails scraped their tender skin. For obvious reasons the house saw many tenants come and go until an elderly man moved in. He never had any problems with the green lady – she must have only enjoyed terrorising children.

Admittedly there are not many malevolent spirits, but when they are around they can terrorise poor innocent folk like you and me for hundreds and hundreds of years.

A group of monks came from Europe in the Dark Ages and established a monastery in Leeds. At first all seemed well, but after a while people noticed that a lot of young maidens were going missing all the time. Now you might not like your little sister too much but I'm sure you'd be pretty concerned if her and her friends began disappearing from the face of the earth. The locals knew that only one thing had changed recently: the monks had arrived.

One fellow called Tom Moody suspected the monks. He gathered the local villagers around him and set off to investigate. They broke down the abbey doors and were horrified to find the monks sacrificing a young girl in the middle of a devil's pentagram. They weren't monks of god, they were monks of the DEVIL!!!

This was too much for the local lord and the monks were burned alive in the grounds of their abbey. Being devil worshippers and all that, they weren't too happy and cursed the lord, the locals and the location with their dying breaths.

Bad in life, bad in death, bad in the afterlife.

It seemed the monks were reluctant to leave. The lord's descendants suffered bad luck for ever after and the family eventually died out. Little would grow in the surrounding fields and for many years the entire area was deserted.

Then in the 20th Century, Leeds spread out. A developer bought the land and built, of all things, a cinema!

It was the Cinema from Hell. Eventually nobody would work there as doors would slam, lights were turned on and off and the projector caught fire when the building was meant to be empty. Patrons who came to see the latest Charlie Chaplin movies felt clammy hands settle around their throats while others felt that somebody was sitting next to them in the darkness and glaring malevolently at them. Hard to enjoy a comedy movie with all that going on!

The cinema closed down. A new owner took over but one year later the whole thing burnt down. Twenty-five people were burned to death; all were young women. It seems the monks were determined to maintain their sacrifices to the Dark Lord.

The land was abandoned for another forty years before a brewery purchased it. Being a brewery they built a pub. All of the owners felt uncomfortable on the premises and the worst place was the cellar. One publican, called Dick Strange, was down there when he felt that somebody was staring at his back. He turned around just in time to see a cowled monk walk through the wall.

Dick and his wife died when their car burst into flames for no reason. Their daughter died soon after.

The next three publicans were unmarried men and they reported no strange incidents.

The one after them was not so lucky. He had a beautiful wife and two equally lovely 19-year-old twin daughters. All of them died when the pub burnt down three months later. The only thing left was a pentagram drawn on the cellar floor!

POLTERGEISTS

Many poltergeists seem to be malevolent and delight in chucking stuff about and causing a whole lot of trouble. I personally think that they are quite often ordinary people throwing things around and hoping not to be seen. Poltergeists are meant to attach themselves to teenage girls and boys because they are so emotional – I live with three teenagers and believe me they cause much more trouble than any rubbish old poltergeist ever could!

If you're a poltergeist reading this, come and prove me wrong! Come on, I dare you!

I must admit I have had one poltergeist experience. It was my first real experience with the supernatural.

While studying in university I lived on the top floor of a two-storey house near the centre of town. I was living with my girlfriend at the time but things weren't going particularly well in the relationship. Things got even worse when a school friend suggested that he move in as we had a spare room. I thought 'What a great idea, it will save on rent and we'll have a great time together.'

My good buddy then started to forget paying his rent and emptied the fridge of any food. Fortunately, you guys don't have to worry about this kind of stuff yet but once I realised that I had been played I was not too happy.

One fine morning I was sitting at the kitchen table minding my own business. I was chowing down on some two-minute noodles (I was a student remember). My girlfriend was pretty arty and loved old stuff. On the table was a nice vase and a couple of glasses from the fifties. You may have seen the type of glass in charity shops. They have gold rims, red or blue patterned lines, and frosting on the bottom half.

My old mate ███████████ (name deleted for legal reasons) came into the kitchen and walked towards the table. One of the frosted glasses, which was about three feet away from me and four from ██████████ (name deleted for legal reasons), lifted up from the table and hovered about eight feet in the air. It then zoomed up to where the ceiling met the wall and tapped on the top, before sliding down the wall and resting gently on the floor.

JJ Moore's first brush with the supernatural. Explain that!

Now that is not the kind of thing you expect to see every day. Pretty amazing. But what is really astonishing is that █████████ and I looked at the glass, watched it on its journey and then looked directly at each other.

We didn't say a thing. What was there to say? 'Wow did you see that glass lift off?' We both saw it plain as day and that was all there was to it.

Poltergeist activity is meant to happen when emotions are at their highest. Maybe our conflicting thoughts caused the glass to fly up and slide down the wall. But it could have been something else entirely – perhaps a spirit that *didn't* like conflict.

GHOSTLY PETS

My grandmother had a lovely dachshund who she loved very dearly. After 15 years the poor little sausage passed away, but late at night she'd hear him scratching and scritching at the back door, wanting to be let in, just like he had done thousands of times before. I'm not sure whether this was an old lady's fancy or something that really happened, but it seems to fit the pattern of pet hauntings. People hear their animal running around or see it out playing in the garden or maybe running up the stairs as if it was still alive. Most of these stories are pretty harmless.

Most.

A young family moved into a housing estate near Portsmouth in England. They had two children. One was a four-year-old boy and the other was a baby girl who was too young to crawl. Both children slept in the nursery on the first floor. The boy slept in his bed next to his baby sister's cot.

At first the family settled into their new home well. However, after a few months the young lad started asking about the 'little fluffy white dog'. His parents asked him what he meant and they were told by the four-year-old that when he went to bed he would sometimes be woken up by the little dog sleeping at the end of his bed. 'The dog makes my feet cold,' he said to his parents.

The parents weren't too concerned, even though the boy often spoke of the dog. Sometimes it slept in the wardrobe, sometimes behind the toy box and occasionally under the baby's cot.

Two months later the family had a tragedy. The baby died. It was diagnosed with SIDS – Sudden Infant Death Syndrome. This is a mysterious disease that still affects many children around the world.

Many weeks after the funeral the sad parents noticed that their son wasn't mentioning the little white dog anymore. They asked him if he had seen it lately. The boy replied, 'No. I haven't seen him since the night he went to sleep on baby's face. That was the night she went to join Grandma in heaven.'

SPOOKY!!!

HAUNTINGS – SPIRITS LEFT BEHIND

The most reliable stories about hauntings seem to involve somebody who has died and seems reluctant to leave their house or work. Either the ghosts don't know they are dead or they just don't want to leave because they had so much fun there. What is pretty amazing about these stories is the way different people who don't even know each other experience the same thing, often over a period of years.

Don't give this pet to your baby brother!

An old house in the woods near Mishawaka Indiana was a beautiful two-storey residence with two large bedrooms on the top floor. A young girl called Pam had one room while her cousin Roberta had the one next door. Both rooms had lovely built in wardrobes.

One night Pam was drifting off to sleep when she heard a strange rustling sound coming from her wardrobe. It was a full moon so she could see quite clearly. She sat up and looked towards where the sound came from and saw a hunched, dark shadow moving slowly across the room. The shape seemed to make a strange rasping noise, as if it was having trouble breathing. The shape slowly glided past the foot of Pam's bed before disappearing out of her door. The young girl was of course terrified (I would be too!). She pulled her quilt over her head and, after what seemed like an eternity, drifted off to sleep.

Even ghosts can run out of breath.

I'm sure you've had an amazing dream that is so good that it wakes you up and you are sure you will remember it forever. In the middle of the night you might promise yourself to write it down first thing in the morning. But then when you wake up it's kind of difficult to remember what it was all about and it doesn't seem nearly as important.

Well that's just like Pam felt the next day when she went down to breakfast, and she half convinced herself that the whole creepy shape thing was just part of her imagination. She decided not to bring it up and tucked into the pile of pancakes her mum put down for breakfast.

Cousin Roberta came and joined the family, and to Pam's amazement she began talking about a strange figure who had moved through her room making a disturbing gasping noise. Pam immediately relived all she had seen and the family were amazed at the similarity of the stories.

Pam's mum had by this time gone quite pale. She knew that the previous owner had been an old woman who suffered from arthritis as well as chronic asthma. She had passed away in Pam's room while dressing for bed. The girls noticed the mother's shocked expression and after much nagging she told them the whole story.

The ghost did not appear again to the girls. No doubt it was checking out that the new owners were doing the right thing for the house.

Several years later the older brother came home to the house after a football game. He had several friends with him and as they walked up the stairs they all saw a strange mist in front of Pam's bedroom. While they were fearless when going for a football, the strange mist was too much for them all and they took off at full speed.

While the previous story seems to describe an old lady who was attached to her house and didn't want to move on, other spirits seem to hang around because they don't know they are dead.

I'm not sure if spirits are awake and aware all the time. Maybe they are awake 24–7 but can only make themselves known to us at special times under certain circumstances. Or else maybe they can only appear to special people who have 'second sight' or a 'sixth sense'.

I would hope that these lost spirits are not always aware. It would be a pretty horrible experience wandering around wondering what you were doing there, looking at people going about their daily life and not being able to communicate and say g'day.

In Becontree Station in the London Underground there seems to be a passenger who is trying to get out of the station.

One station supervisor was working the late shift during the 1990s. The supervisor had to finish some paperwork before he could go home and was sitting in the office at the lower platform. The office had one main door to the main platform and another door to the side that gave access to the National Line platform – a door that was seldom used. As he worked, the supervisor heard this door handle rattle several times. Entering into the man's subconscious was the thought that the National Line train was approaching. He continued working, but several minutes later the door rattled again. Strange, he thought, that train went through several minutes ago. He continued working.

Three or four minutes later the door handle rattled again. No question – something was wrong. There was another station guard at a higher level and the supervisor was by now thoroughly unnerved and wanted some human company. He left the office, locking the door behind him, and proceeded along the deserted platform towards the empty escalator. While walking he had an uncanny feeling that somebody was staring at the back of his head.

He turned and saw the figure of a young woman. She was wearing a pink blouse with a long white skirt. She had long blonde hair that went almost to her waist. There seemed to be a despairing intensity coming from the figure but the supervisor could not tell what expression she had. The young woman didn't have a face – just an opaque flat surface surrounded by hair.

In what seemed an instant, she was gone. The rail man turned and dashed up the escalator to find his companion.

'You look like you've seen a ghost!' exclaimed his colleague. 'Was she blonde with a white dress? I've seen her too.'

He explained that many of the station's staff had seen her over the years and she was always on the Eastern Line platform.

Overtime isn't always pleasant at Becontree Station.

Twelve years earlier a train had been leaving Becontree when there was a horrible accident that killed 24 passengers.

Maybe the young blonde lady died so suddenly she didn't realise she had even left the platform. Maybe she wanders, confused, trying to leave the station. Occasionally she finds a guard and tries to get their attention.

All of the reported sightings have been made by railway workers. She has never appeared to members of the public.

CHILD GHOSTS

I don't mean actual ghosts of children, but ghosts who appear to children and nobody else.

Maybe when you were a tiny tot you were more receptive to seeing the supernatural. As you get older your mind gets clogged up with meaningless stuff like PlayStation, Xbox, Nintendo and homework. After a while members of the opposite sex will take up another 90%.

But when you were young there was perhaps enough room for the supernatural to slip in.

A good friend of mine called Patricia raised three children in a house in the hills just beyond the city limits. The house was quite old and had the usual range of creaks and bangs that are normally found in old houses with worn out plumbing and woodwork.

Patricia had three daughters and the youngest was called Emily. Emily had a cute little habit. Quite often when she came to visit her mum and dad in their bedroom she would look up into the back corner and giggle and laugh. Occasionally she even pointed into the corner. This lasted for several years, but by the time Emily turned seven or eight it stopped. Many years later, when all of Patricia's children had got jobs and moved out, Patricia and her husband decided that the house was too big and that they would sell it and buy something smaller.

It's hard to get Generation Z off their tech.

A willing buyer was soon found and on the day before they moved out of the house the whole family reunited to help with the packing. After a hard day's work, they were all seated around the dinner table surrounded by full packing crates. As they drank their cups of tea Emily had a question for her mum.

'Mum, do you remember how you and dad shared the top bedroom?' she asked.

Her mother replied, 'Of course dear, why do you ask?'

'I wonder who that old lady was who was always crouching up near your ceiling. She always seemed very pleased to see me and would make funny faces and wave at me. When I wasn't there she always seemed very sad and would just look out of the window. She had a long face and I could never see her eyes.'

Only Emily could see her parents' visitor.

42

Of course Patricia was pretty taken aback after hearing that story. She and her husband were pleased that they only had to spend one more night in the old family home. I'm not sure if she told the new owners what Emily had seen.

Every year on the anniversary of a big battle some poor news reporter is sent out to report on a bunch of re-enactors recreating the historical event. The most famous one is Waterloo, but there are 'living historians' who recreate all periods. These include Vikings, American Civil War soldiers and medieval fighters. No doubt you've seen these characters and been astounded how most of them were fat, middle-aged men!

Many of these people are absolutely devoted to the hobby and spend every spare moment following their passion.

No one was more dedicated to firing off muskets and living in teepees than Tipper McLean. Every year he'd turn up to the Taminick firing range, 200 kilometres out of town, for a big re-enacting event during the September holidays. Tipper's particular passion was living the life of an American trapper in the Great Lakes region around about the early 18th Century. These Mountain Men wore buckskin clothes, raccoon hats and almost always had long bushy beards.

Tipper also had a passion for the American War of Independence and was a dab hand at shooting targets with his ancient matchlock – especially if the target looked like a British redcoat.

Tipper passed away several years ago. His will was pretty unusual. He wanted his cremains to be fired out of a cannon. Cremains are the left over ashes from a dead body once it has been cremated. The fire does not destroy teeth and some bones. Once the burnt bits are cooled, the funeral parlour man grinds these solid bits into a fine ash.

Tipper wasn't fired into the afterlife.

So one chilly morning a six pounder cannon was hauled up to the Taminick firing range and a charge of powder was rammed down the barrel. Tipper's remains followed, powder was placed down the touch hole and BAM! He was discharged at a muzzle velocity of one thousand and four hundred feet per second!

That would be enough to finish off most people, but Tipper still hangs around the camping ground. Many people have reported footsteps walking next to them at the dead of night even though nobody can be seen. Other re-enactors have lost things but some presence has helpfully found the missing item and tossed it back at them.

One person has seen Tipper.

The mornings at the firing range are usually terrifically chilly, so most people stay in their warm sleeping bags for as long as possible. One morning, as mist rolled over the lower campground, a fellow was woken by his son, who had to use the conveniences. He took the five-year-old to do his business and carried along his water can so he could fill it up at the same time.

While he was crouching down to fill the can his son tugged his sleeve. 'Hey Dad, who's that old man up there?' The father looked up, but he couldn't see anything and brushed his son off.

'Dad he's waving at us, up at the gate.' Approximately 150 yards away was the entrance to the upper camp, but try as he might the boy's father could only see a gate!

The young boy described the old man he saw. Suddenly it dawned on the experienced camper and a cold shiver ran up his spine: it was an exact description of Tipper McLean, complete with long grey beard and raccoon hat.

The old Mountain Man was obviously pleased that at least some folk were out braving the cold morning air.

One of the most haunted sites in England is found at the Derby Branch of the National Bank. The bank was built over a maze of old passageways and cells that used to be part of the Derby jail. This jail was built hundreds of years ago and many people were hanged outside the jail in the town square. The building was eventually demolished and the Derby National Bank branch was built there.

Ever since it opened in the 1970s strange things were reported. Bank clerks doing their sums would look at their calculators and find that extra numbers had been added into their calculations. Lights were turned on and off even when the only person in the bank was the security guard.

The ghost was obviously mischievous. Customers and bank staff often heard footsteps, laughter and the sound of singing. In-trays and out-trays would be tipped over, and on occasion the wheeled mop bucket would whizz by, splashing water all over the marble tiles. Heavy paperweights would be swept off the desk while nobody was looking and things would go missing only to appear later in the unlikeliest of places.

While adults in the bank can only see the effects of the haunting, some children have been able to see the ghost.

One young mother was standing in line and noticed that her little boy was starting to cry. She asked him what the matter was, and her son pointed towards one of the desks where customers fill in their deposit and withdrawal slips. He explained that he had rolled his rubber ball to the little boy who was hiding under the desk, but the boy was refusing to roll it back. The mum peered in the direction that her son was pointing but couldn't see anything. She was about to tell her son not to be silly when he said, 'Mum, the boy says he will give me the ball back if he can come to our place for dinner. It's very cold where he lives and he is often very lonely.' He then described how the urchin was clothed in rags and seemed to be so cold that his skin had turned almost blue.

Other children have reported the spirit peering around corners or looking down from the top floor stairs.

Surprisingly the ghost also shows himself to little old ladies and has even been reported to tug on their skirts to get their attention.

Some ghosts don't know they're ghosts!

JAIL GHOSTS

Not surprisingly, in many jails where executions were carried out there are frequent reports of spooky goings on.

In the notorious Long Bay Jail in NSW, a prisoner who was confined in cell 47 in 4 wing complained to the guard. He was kept awake at night by strange goings on and unexplained noises. In jails there is always a background noise of clanging and banging, but in the dead of night it was almost as if somebody was whispering in the prisoner's ear. He could never make out any clear sentences, but a steady anxious murmuring was there whenever he closed his eyes.

That was not all. The temperature would unexpectedly plunge, even on the hottest of days. The guard pointed out to the frightened prisoner the welded metal square two meters from the cell. He explained that it was the old trapdoor used to hang more than twenty prisoners. Cells 47 and 48 had been the condemned cells for many years. The helpful guard pointed out a large wooden beam suspended above the old trap door. It was from this beam that the deadly noose had been suspended.

Cell 47 obviously had more than one permanent resident.

Newgate Prison in London has a shade that is seen late at night. A little old lady carrying a small bundle that looks like a carefully wrapped baby wanders around the corridors and even into the

'C'mon, guv'nor, I thought I was in solitary!'

warden's office. But this is not a harmless little old lady. It might be the ghost of Amelia Dyer – England's worst mass murderer.

Amelia had a tragic life and her family had a history of being a bit 'crackerjack' (nuts – not a medical term). She went from job to job but finally found her true vocation as a 'baby farmer'. Hundreds of years ago it was seen as a real shame for young women to get pregnant before they were married. The choice was to have a very dangerous abortion or else go into 'confinement', have the baby and give it up for adoption. The baby farmer's job was to arrange the adoption and care for the little mites until a new home could be found. They received a considerable payment for this service.

But Amelia found a more profitable method. She took the young kiddie. She took the young mother's money. And then she took the young kiddie's life by wrapping it tight and strangling it with a ribbon. It seems she took up to 400 young souls and would carry the sad little bundles down to the River Thames, where she threw them in the water. She was caught and hanged on 10 June 1896, at Newgate Prison.

But, for whatever reason, she has not left the prison and glides silently around the corridors at night holding her little bundle. Maybe she is looking for a river so that she can dispose of one final baby! I once took a tour of Newgate and I'm rather glad to say I didn't come across Amelia.

Pentridge Prison in Victoria was the home of many horrible, horrible people who committed all kinds of crimes. In D wing the gallows still remain. Many criminals were hanged on this large beam of wood, but that does not necessarily mean they have all left. If you take a photo in the damp, echoing corridors there is a fair chance you will take a picture of a shadowman – one of the many prisoners who refuse to leave.

JAPANESE GHOSTS

The Japanese aren't only great at making cars – they also make some of the scariest horror movies. The dead scary ghosts found in movies such as *The Grudge* and *The Eye* aren't recent inventions, but in fact have terrorised Japanese society for thousands of years.

The Japanese are like the Chinese in that they believe that before a soul can move on after death there must be a properly conducted funeral. If this is observed the soul becomes a friendly spirit, which returns once a year during the Obon festival to receive offerings and cast a kindly look over the family.

But if the person dies violently or the rites aren't carried out properly it becomes an angry spirit called a yūrei (translates literally to 'hazy spirit').

The yūrei thirsts for revenge and can use its emotions of hatred or sorrow to re-enter the physical world and wreak havoc on those left behind. The most dangerous kind of yūrei is one that learns to love terrorising innocent people and causing as much murder and mayhem as possible. Only when the correct rites are performed or the conflict that led to the death is resolved will the enraged spirit find peace.

The yūrei are very scary to look at. They are dressed in a flowing white robe (a burial shroud) and have an almost white, pale face with deep black bags under their eyes. The hair is long, black and dishevelled, just as if it has been lying underground for several

Don't attract the attention of a yūrei, whatever you do.

years. Yūrei float around with their arms outstretched and their hands dangling uselessly from the wrist. They have to float because these nasty spirits lack legs or feet.

Not all Japanese ghosts are bad. An ubume is the spirit of a mother who died in childbirth. She returns to look after her children and even gives them sweets. Zashiki-warashi are the ghosts of children. They are not usually evil but can be very mischievous.

POSSIBLE CAUSES

It is funny that most people I have talked to about ghosts say that they never believed in them … until they saw one. There seem to be quite a few theories about what causes ghosts. One of my favourite theories accounts for the classic haunting in an old house.

Think of the classic ghost story. It is a windy night with thunder and rain and wind gusts whining through the trees. The weather shakes windows and doors in an old house and gradually the inhabitants develop a feeling of foreboding as if something is not right. Suddenly a crash of thunder and a flash of lightning lights up a bedroom and there, standing in the corner of the room, is an old hag with staring eyes and outstretched claws. Another flash and the hag has moved closer to the terrified inhabitant – and now she has a maniacal leer revealing what seem to be sharpened fangs.

Invariably the poor person collapses in a faint or hides under their bedding until dawn.

Well there might be a perfectly scientific explanation for this. Sometimes in this situation it is just a shadowy figure seen out of the corner of the eye, or else maybe a sound of footsteps or laughter – these could all be auditory or visual hallucinations.

Well, what could bring them on? The answer is … magic mushrooms!

Many different kinds of mushrooms and fungi have the power to alter our minds. Old houses have lots of damp dark places where mushrooms flourish. The mushrooms breed by releasing tiny spores and they love windy conditions so that the spores can be spread far and wide. Just like coral, they often all let their spores go at the same time.

Some ghosts might be produced by our minds.

Maybe on a windy night in an old, damp house, the inhabitants breathe in thousands of millions of tiny spores without even knowing it, and these spores then cause hallucinations.

The other commonly held theory is that vibrations that we cannot hear are causing our body to react in mysterious ways that lead to hallucinations. Elephants for example can communicate with members of their herds even though they are miles away. They do this by using subsonic frequencies that are too low for our ears to hear. Dog whistles operate on a similar principal, being too high for us to hear.

The theory runs that although we cannot actually hear the sounds they are disturbing our inner ear and setting up patterns that our mind then turns into images or sounds that are mildly disturbing or spooky. The theory runs that overactive imaginations turn these funny sensations into voices, nausea and apparitions. Apparitions are classed as a corner-of-the-eye phenomenon, which is when there seems to be a moving figure just out of your range of vision. As you turn to look, it is gone.

Hundreds of haunted houses, pubs and castles have cellars. These tend to be the sites of most common hauntings. They are also where subsonic noises are likely to occur. Underground tunnels and underground earth movements are the most likely causes of subsonic frequencies.

There is one more theory which a lot paranormal investigators believe in: that of the 'stone recorder'. This idea says that when there are really strong emotions they are somehow absorbed or recorded by the surrounding environment. Some examples of these emotional events include when a young girl has her heart broken, when there is a dreadful murder … or when your little brother is asked to clean up his room! There is so much anger or emotion that it rings out like a bell to make a permanent recording. Over the ages this recording plays back time after time after time.

People who support this theory reckon that when people are present their emotions trigger the recording so that it plays back. They also think that the recording fades over time. When a ghost appears soon after they die the recording is strong and might include loud voices and full body apparitions. As time passes these apparitions fade until they are just shadows, or even body parts like walking legs. The sounds get weaker too. What once was a noise that echoed down the hallway for all to hear becomes a whisper or murmur that is only heard in the dead of night.

Eventually the ghost just fades away and is never seen or heard again.

Some scientists think ghosts are recordings.

The stone recorder theory accounts for apparitions that repeat the same actions time after time after time – but not for ghosts that interact with people.

There is one more theory that is a little out there. I made up this theory so I'd be interested to know what you think. I call it the 'Fart Cushion Theory'. What if ghosts are just dead people who have a sense of humour and want to hang around causing as much mayhem as possible? A lot of hauntings are pretty much practical jokes: pulling blankets off sleeping people, moving stuff around or hiding it, creeping up on people and pulling their hair, poking when it's not expected, walking up to a door in the dead of night and turning the door handle before vanishing, turning off lights … and so on.

Maybe after a good haunting the ghosts crack up laughing and compare who had the best trick.

'Did you see the look on so-and-so's face? I thought he was going to wet himself.'

'That's nothing, that young fellow turned whiter than a bed sheet and knocked four old ladies over as he headed for the exit.'

What's scarier, a clown or a clown ghost?

CHAPTER 3

LIFE SUCKS – SO DOES DEATH!

Does this sound familiar?

You have a beautiful younger sister. She seems to be the life of the party. Most younger sisters and brothers are an awful pain. But your sister has such a sweet nature that you can forget that your parents obviously love her more and that she doesn't always do her fair share of the jobs (she never picks up the steaming, warm dog poo in a plastic bag when you take Wags for a walk for example).

Anyway we won't go on about that. Although she is sometimes a royal P.I.T.A. (Pain In The … Ankle) you love your sister.

One morning you notice that things are changing. You used to hear her laughter ringing out in the morning. Her pink cheeks were always smiling with the cutest dimple ever. Now she seems to be a bit pale. She spends a lot of time in her bedroom and you hardly hear her. At dinner everybody tucks into pizza or fried rice, but 'sis' just toys with her food.

Over the next few months she becomes pale and skinny. Her eyes become sunken. She seems to have difficulty breathing. It is even harder for her to get out of bed and most of the day is spent sleeping. She has difficulty going out into the sunlight and has to shield her eyes from bright light.

Even her lips seem to shrink so that her teeth start to look a bit fang-like.

Suddenly you realise – she's turning into a vampire!!!

This story isn't made up – it is true. In the 1900s this happened thousands and thousands of times in England and Europe and even America. But what the poor young people were suffering from was not Vampirism but Tuberculosis; we call it TB.

Sign up to be a vampire today.

Another name for TB was 'consumption'. This was because it seemed to 'consume' people slowly over a long period of time. We now know that a nasty little bacteria gets into people's lungs and makes them waste away. Back then people did not know this and came up with another cause: vampires. They thought that every night a vampire would sneak into young people's bedrooms and suck a bit of their blood and life force out until the poor person wasted away. They were then buried.

But of course, being a vampire meant that they came back from the dead and began to infect other people.

This may seem a bit strange to us but TB was the greatest killer at the time and hundreds of thousands and millions of people died from this dreadful disease.

Maybe, just maybe, some were real vampires!

There was one incident in 1892 when a young lady called Mercy Brown caught the disease and died. Soon after this the rest of her family, especially Mercy's young brother, began to waste away. Her neighbours in New England, America, thought that Mercy was coming back to infect her family and would soon attack the rest of the community. They stormed into Mercy's crypt and tore off the dead girl's coffin lid. Remarkably, she still looked just like she did when she died (maybe not so remarkable what with it being winter and all and her body being frozen).

That was not all. Sometimes dead bodies do a little 'belly burp'. The gasses in their bodies force a bit of blood out of their mouths to cover their lips and run down the chin. It makes them look as if they have just had a good feed of blood. Mercy's lips were covered in blood. The neighbours were so scared they cut out her heart and burnt it. They then forced Mercy's sick brother to eat the ashes.

Not surprisingly, he died soon afterwards.

VAMPIRES IN HISTORY

The earliest civilisations all believed in vampires. Even as long as 5,000 years ago the Ancient Sumerians thought there were mysterious creatures that flew around at night sucking the blood from innocent victims. The Babylonians believed in the Lilitu. It was a flying demon and particularly loved the blood of babies.

The Ancient Greeks loved their vampires so much that they had two kinds; the Lamia loved sucking on the blood of young children while the Striges would attack grown-ups.

They also told the story of a young man called Ambrogio who was very much like a vampire even though he was not called one.

He did a lot of things wrong so that gods made him allergic to silver. If he was exposed to direct sunlight Ambrogio's skin would burn and splinter. But another god took pity on him. She gave the young man superhuman strength, immortality, fangs that allowed him to drink blood and the power to make anybody like him if they drank his blood.

ASIAN VAMPIRES

Vampires are found throughout Asia and some of them are the scariest creatures you will ever experience. In Japan, Malaysia and even Indonesia they have a horrific creature that loves sucking blood. During the day they look like beautiful young woman but at night the creatures turn into horrible old hags with sharp yellow teeth and long hollow tongues. If that is not bad enough, these creatures have heads that fly off their bodies and whizz around searching for an open window. They particularly like feeding off young children and will fly through bedroom windows and use their sharp tongue to cut into the children's veins. They then suck up the blood with lots of slurping sounds.

That's all pretty gross but these manananggal (separating demons) also love the taste of the snot, phlegm and vomit of sick people.

Indonesians had a particularly nasty kind of vampire. These undead creatures looked like beautiful, long-haired young women. But the long hair covered a hole on the back of their neck filled with razor sharp fangs. They would lure little children into the forests. When nobody was looking the matianak's head would swivel around, showing the horrible mouth. The matianak then grabbed the kiddie-wink and sucked out all of its blood!

These might sound pretty scary but they've got nothing on the Malaysian Penanggalan. This lady vampire has a head and dangling from her neck is a stomach sac and nothing else!!! She only feeds on tiny babies and flies around at night looking for them.

FUN FACT
THE REAL DRACULA
. . . .

No doubt you've heard about Vlad Dracula – was he all that bad? Why has one of the evilest monsters ever been named after Vlad?

It could be because his surname, which he inherited from his dad, means 'Son of the Devil'. So really he was the son of the devil who was son of the devil.

Let's have a look at what he did. Vlad's old man, who was king of Wallachia, was killed by the local nobles. Vlad then became the king but he had to fight against all kinds of enemies.

He tried to frighten them off, so he decided to impale everybody he could. Impaling is a particularly nasty way of being killed. A big stake, kind of like a satay stick on steroids, is forced up the bum of a poor victim before it is hammered into the ground. Vlad made an art form of it and loved experimenting. Sometimes whole families were stuck on the one stake. Parents would be on the bottom and kiddie-winks on top. Sometimes the stake went through the mouth so the poor bugger was facing downwards.

Vlad did this to anybody he could get his hands on: women, children, Turks, Hungarians and even his own Wallachians.

Vlad took such pleasure in it that he used to have lunch surrounded by a forest of impaled people. He had a steak while they all had stake.

Eventually Vlad's own family realised that they would soon run out of people to rule, so they booted old Vlad out and locked him in prison. Vlad didn't mind too much – he spent his time impaling rats and mice and bugs that he found in his cell!

So was Vlad really all that bad?

Yes. He was born bad.

BECOMING A VAMPIRE

There are lots of ways of becoming a vampire. Some experts think that if a vampire feeds on a person and drains every last bit of blood then the victim will die. But if the vampire leaves a bit of blood in their veins, so that their heart keeps beating, then the person will become a vampire.

Others think that to become a vampire you need to suck a vampire's blood or have it injected.

Whatever the method, all experts agree that it is a painful process. Since every bit of their body has to transform into a blood-sucking, super strong, immortal freak, every single cell has to die before it is reinvented.

Some cultures think that people are born to be vampires. There are ways to tell if your baby is a vampire. If they are born with teeth, that is a dead giveaway. Also babies with a third nipple or a split lower lip were seen as evil-omened and possibly returned from the dead.

Vampires that have not been 'turned' for long are always quite human-like and can be mistaken for a normal person. But as they get older they tend to look creepier and creepier. Their skin gets paler, their arms and legs get longer and skinnier, their eyes turn redder and their fangs get longer and longer until they almost reach down to the vampire's chin!

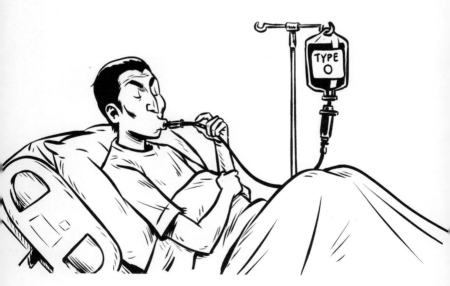

There's no cure for vampirism.

65

Old vampires even lose the power of speech. The only sounds they make will be a terrifying shriek, as they pounce on their prey, and a low slobbering moan as they drain every last bit of blood.

Old vampires are the most scary. There are no human feelings left and the only pleasure they get is from sucking the blood out of any poor person that they come across.

FINDING A VAMPIRE

Since people were so scared of vampires they made sure there were a whole lot of ways to find them. There are lots of dead giveaways (maybe they should be called *un*dead giveaways). Vampires avoid mirrors because they can't cast a reflection. They can't enter a house unless they are actually invited in. They hate garlic bread and love to sleep all day.

The best way to find a vampire is to place a young boy on a

white horse and get them to walk around a graveyard at night. The horse will stop at a grave and if you dig it up you will be sure to find a vampire. It will have grey skin, long claws and probably blood around its mouth.

If you come across a vampire at night you can keep it off you by waving a cross in front of it or sprinkling holy water or rosemary on it. This will make the vampire hiss and splutter and hopefully turn into a bat and fly away.

KILLING VAMPIRES

For some reason there are not a lot of tips on how to be nice to a vampire. This is no doubt because they are bloodthirsty, blood-sucking, evil, undead creatures that only want to kill as many humans as possible.

Here are some suggested methods for getting rid of a vampire:

- When you bury a vampire, pound a wooden stake through its heart, mouth or stomach. Best to be on the safe side and do all three.
- Pound metal stakes through their neck, groin and ankles before burying the vampire.
- Cover a buried vampire with sharp scythes over their body. When the vampire tries to rise it will cut itself into pieces.
- Put a brick in the mouth of the vampire. It will not be able to get out of the grave until it chews through the brick – like, never.
- Place sand in the grave. This keeps the vampire busy as it has to count the grains of sand before it can leave the grave. It can only count one grain a year so when it does finally emerge it will be somebody else's problem.

- Chop off the vampire's head and put it under its bum or between its legs. I'm not sure why this was done but it would sure be unpleasant to wake up with your nose up your bum.
- Gypsies used to place iron needles in the vampire's heart, mouth and over its eyes.
- Pour boiling water over the grave.
- Put a lemon in the mouth of the vampire before burial.
- Shoot bullets through the coffin.
- Chop the vampire up, boil it and then burn all of the pieces.

CHAPTER 4

WARNINGS FROM THE DEAD

The banshee has been around for at least 1,000 years. Her role is to warn a family that a loved one will soon die, using her scary keening or wailing voice.

Since they have been evolving for so many years, there are many kinds of banshee. I am sure you would agree it wouldn't be too bad to see a beautiful silver-haired lady gently sobbing and crying. This is one form of banshee and she often appears close to woods and fields or in dreams. Despite the fact that the message is pretty horrible, at least the delivery wouldn't be too shocking.

Many banshees are much scarier. Sometimes they look like scary old crones with bright red burning eyes and long fingernails that are more like talons. These frightful horrors pursue their victims, all the while letting out blood curdling shrieks that can stop a man's heart in terror. Others are merely wrinkled old women with rotten teeth and grey hair who moan and sob. They move away when approached but many of these hags have a comb stuck in their hair – a symbol of bad luck.

Probably the most frightening banshee is the figure of a headless, naked old hag with saggy breasts reaching down almost to her knees and carrying an earthenware pot full of blood. How she manages to scream and carry on without a head is not explained but it's certainly not a sight that I'd like to wake up to!

Other banshees appear outside a doomed person's house and it is usually said that only the immediate family can hear the dire warning.

More often than not you cannot see a banshee but only hear the wail, floating eerily on a breeze. Such was the case of a young university student in Dublin: Tom O'Shea.

When you are in university you might find yourself in the fortunate position of living in a dormitory so that you can spend time studying with your pals. At the end of the 19th Century one young man from an ancient Irish family was studying with his friends in the loft of University College. As midnight approached, Tom's friends noticed that he was looking anxious and drawn. They tried to continue concentrating on their studies, but all of a sudden Tom leapt up from the table and dashed towards the window, throwing it open and letting in the cold night air.

The young man leaned out into the air and asked his friends to be quiet.

'Shoosh. Can you hear anything?' he asked. Tom's friends joined him at he windows but could hear nothing, only the occasional clatter of a horse-drawn carriage or the low murmurs of students returning to their dormitories.

Knots can put even the nicest banshee in a bad mood.

'Can you hear that long wail? There! It is louder when the wind blows in this direction. It is surely the bean sídhe. Is she singing for me or for someone else?'

Bean sídhe is the Irish name for a banshee.

Tom's friends comforted the anxious student and when they saw him the next morning he appeared to have recovered his cheerful mood. The group of friends proceeded to the first lecture of the day, but soon after it had commenced a professor interrupted the proceedings and summoned Tom to his office. The professor had bad news. He had just received a telegraph declaring that Mrs O'Shea, Tom's mother, had died the previous night on the stroke of midnight.

Bean sídhe is one name given to the banshee, but there are many others; the Scales Crow, the Bow, She Devil and the Babd are all common names.

She does not always predict a family member's death. In 1866 a Dublin paper told the story of Mary Lincoln, who had a scary experience returning home from her position in the local pub. As usual in the days before electricity, it was a pitch black evening.

It's not always a good idea to follow a banshee.

There was a fair wind and clouds scudded above, blocking out any moonlight. Mary was used to this and had walked the way countless times. Just as she crossed a small bridge the wailing of the wind seemed to take on a life of its own, until she could hear a desperate keening. The cry of distress grew louder and Mary made out the shape of a hunched old lady 30 feet in front of her. Mary went to comfort the women but, in a split second, the figure seemed to leap ahead out of Mary's grasp. The serving girl was a good hearted soul and tried to catch up, but the woman vanished into the darkness, her keening and wailing getting more desperate all the time. The last Mary heard was one more piteous shriek as the woman disappeared up the hill towards Old Shanashea's farm.

That was well out of her way and Mary continued on her original route. Soon she was at home warming up in front of the fire and telling the story to her grandfather.

While he said nothing that evening, the grandfather gathered some neighbours and at first light they walked down to the crossroads before heading up to Shanashea's farm. At first they couldn't locate the man, until some bright spark looked in the well. There they found their neighbour. Whether he had thrown himself into the well, whether he stumbled in by accident or whether he had been pursued by the banshee, they could not be sure, but when Shanashea was hauled up into the daylight his features were frozen into a rictus of terror.

In some parts of Ireland it is advised to stand still while a banshee is letting off steam. Otherwise death for the witness can result.

Of course the banshee is an Irish wraith, but throughout Europe there are many other harbingers of death. For some reason many are reported as having saucers for eyes. Black hounds, donkeys, horses, bulls

WUF!

Beware the crockery-spaniel.

and even chickens have been reported. In the dead of night, a solitary traveller can be minding his own business until he hears a mighty screech and onto the road or track leaps an animal. Where the eyes are supposed to be there are instead two bright saucers of white light.

I'd sure as heck do a bolt if I saw a ravening dog coming at me with saliva-flecked fangs and bright lights for eyes.

If it was an angry chicken coming at me, clucking angrily, I'm not quite so sure.

In Wicklow Town, England, there is a White Lady of High Street. Any who see her should count themselves fortunate, because they have been given three days to sort out stuff before they drop dead. Biting issues, such as who would inherit the stamp collection and how much of the cutlery would Aunty Mavis get her hands on, could all be conveniently organised.

Scottish folk did not want to see an old woman washing bloody rags in the river. It was 'all over red rover' for you if you did.

Where do banshees come from? Some say that women who die in childbirth often turn into banshees.

Many different cultures have fearsome critters that foretell a not so happy ending:

THE GRAVE SOW Scandinavians believe in a little piglet rooting around a graveyard.

THE WICHTLEIN This ugly little goblin gives its scary message by knocking three times on a bed head.

THE MOTHMAN A winged human-like figure with bright red eyes swoops around the doomed person's head.

CIGUAPA This blue-skinned young woman is any South American's worst enemy.

OWLS Seen in many cultures, including India and Europe, as a deadly omen.

BLACK CATS The Germans believed that if you were sick and a black cat jumped on your bed, there would be no recovery. If one crossed your path while attending a funeral you'd soon join your relative underground.

DEATH If you happen to see a skeleton in a black cowl holding a scythe you've either been reading too much Terry Pratchett or you're about to die.

There is one more kind of banshee, which is confined to a small town in Australia. It is a horse banshee: the Black Horse of Sutton.

One fine day a farmer from Sutton in New South Wales rode into nearby Goulburn to attend to business. As he turned into the long driveway towards his homestead, the farmer's dogs ran barking to greet him. The farmer, Jack Stibbons, was riding his favourite black stallion. Normally he had this fine beast on a tight rein, but for a split second Stibbons loosened his grip and the horse bucked in fright. Stibbons was hurled to the ground where he died instantly of a broken neck.

Mrs Stibbons was unaware of the accident and she spent many hours waiting for his return. Then, just as night fell, she heard the pounding of the stallion's hooves. She rose to greet her husband, but in the twilight could only see the stallion galloping towards the house. Just before it crashed into the veranda the mighty stallion disappeared.

Mrs Stibbons heard the hooves pass through the house and disappear into the distance. She immediately knew that something was wrong and the locals began a search. The farmer and horse were both found – dead.

In the following years many members of the family died tragic deaths: in war, from snakebite, and even one accidental drowning in the well. Each time, just before the unpleasant death, the inhabitants of Stibbons' farmstead would hear and maybe see the galloping black stallion.

Not all visitors are welcome.

CHAPTER 5

A REAL LIFE HORROR

Not all imaginary animals are fake. Some are real. The werewolf is a creature that used to terrorise medieval European towns for hundreds of years.

Just imagine one fine day in a small German town. Nestled in a valley with woods on one side and a river on the other, all seems peaceful as everybody goes about their simple tasks.

Suddenly you hear a scream down by the waterside.

'Werewolf!' comes the cry. You look down the hill and staggering up towards you from the washing rocks are several young girls, with blood dripping from frightful gashes in their arms, legs and even their fair faces.

I THINK HE WANTS TO PLAY FETCH!

Loping behind them is the village woodcutter. He seems scarcely human. Low dog-like growls are wrenched from his throat and out of his mouth comes a bloody froth which hardly covers sharp canines. His lips are pulled back in a skull-like rictus grin. He staggers from side to side, sometimes seeming to leap forward while at other times he can barely stand upright.

The cry of 'Werewolf!' echoes around the village as the men grab spears, pikes, glaives and crossbows. Pouring out of their houses, they concentrate in a circle around the woodsman. Nothing needs to be said.

The cursed werewolf must be killed.

The men descend on the woodsman and hack him into pieces. Fortunately, no more villagers were bitten.

You can spot a rabid dog or a rabid human a mile away. Huge amounts of phlegm and snot and foamy saliva pour out of their muzzles and nostrils while their eyes are inflamed and red. They are driven absolutely crazy by hydrophobia (a fear of water). They growl and bark and bare their jaws, even if there is nobody or nothing near them (kind of like that crazy person on the train who talks to himself). They pant very loudly, are unsteady on their feet and seem to have a glazed look in their little doggy eyes.

While medieval Europeans did not know that the condition was caused by a virus called *rabies lyssavirus*, they knew that once a person showed symptoms there was no hope.

The virus has a particularly cruel method of tormenting its host. When the poor animal or person has been well and truly infected, the virus starts reproducing in huge amounts within the salivary gland. This is of course the place where saliva is created and soon it is full of the nasty little rabies germs determined to infect a new creature. The saliva begins to foam and pour out like a lemonade slushy. The other symptom is hydrophobia, which makes the animal absolutely terrified of even the thought of water and also stops the swallowing reflex.

Infected humans who even think of getting a drink experience painful cramps in the throat.

Back in our village, the men took a breather. They had managed to kill the werewolf without anyone being bitten.

Then they remembered: three girls had fled from the woodsman.

And you thought dogs didn't like baths – try washing a werewolf.

They were covered in blood. Had they been bitten? If they had, there was only one solution!

Rabies has been around for a long time. It seems that dogs first became domesticated maybe hundreds of thousands of years ago and probably the disease has been in humans since then.

Stories of the werewolf have been around for just as long.

THE ORIGINS OF THE LYCANTHROPE

Another word for a shape-shifter is lycanthrope. There are a couple of possibilities for the origin of this word. One Greek myth talks about the horrible King Lycaon, who loved torturing his subjects. The god Zeus heard about the crimes and decided to visit and see if the stories were true. Lycaon worked out who his visitor was and tried to kill him by serving up a heaping of human flesh. Zeus was not to be tricked and destroyed the palace and changed Lycaon into a wolf. Since then the Greek word for wolf was lykos. This was joined with the Greek word anthropos – man – to form the word lycanthrope.

Over the centuries a picture of your standard lycanthrope has emerged. Of course it involves having a lot of hair. Lycanthropes might try to blend into society, but they could be picked out by looking for some common features. When not in wolf form he would have one bushy eyebrow above his eyes rather than two separate ones. Often they had lots of hair in their ears and sticking out of their nostrils, and it was a dead giveaway if they had hairy palms.

They had long and narrow ears and blood red fingernails that were often sharp like talons. They would lick their lips and blink their eyes as if they were thirsty. Werewolves always had a short temper and sometimes had an aversion to sunlight, preferring to stay indoors during the day. Their skin was rough and blotchy, almost like a dog's belly.

Another possible historical explanation for werewolves is that it may be an explanation for those people who we now know as serial killers.

Medieval society was very violent. Peasants and workers were kept in line by brutal knights and an even more brutal legal system. Trial by ordeal was common and outside every town there was a 'crows garrotte'. This was a hollow platform with scaffolds on top. Criminals were hanged and left to rot. Crows would feed on the dead bodies and when bits and pieces started to fall off the town executioner would cut down the dead body and toss it into the central pit.

If the body was mistreated when it was dead, it was nothing compared to what happened to the person when he was alive. Before being executed most crooks were tortured in the town's torture chamber.

With all this violence going on it is no wonder that many people went mad and became horrible serial killers with all of the ferocity of a wolf. Now we think of wolves as rare animals that are only seen in nature documentaries. But in the Middle Ages they were a clear and present danger. Anybody who strayed too far away from the village was likely to be hunted down by a well organised and savage pack of wolves. Villagers knew there were wolves around when they would go into their fields and find bloody bits and pieces of their animals scattered around fields.

When human bits and pieces were found they knew there was another, more dangerous predator around: a werewolf.

FASCINATING FACTS
THE FATAL FULL MOON
· ·

We all know that the event that sets off a full blown werewolf attack is of course a full moon. Well it seems that this isn't just a lot of hooey and there is evidence that a full moon does have an effect on humans and animals and can make them act a bit strange at times. After all, loony and lunatic are both words that come from the Latin word luna, meaning moon.

The full moon messes with everybody's mind.

Doctors at Bradford Royal Infirmary did a survey in 2000 and found that during full moons the number of people they treated for animal bites doubled. Other doctors throughout the world know that their emergency departments are filled with people who have been in fights during the full moon and detectives dread the increased workload that the full moon brings them. You are much more likely to be murdered in a full moon.

In fact some of the worst serial killers in history, such as David Berkowitz, killed most of their victims during a full moon.

PETER STUBBE – THE FIRST WEREWOLF

Near the lovely cathedral town of Cologne around 1591, a lot of young people were going missing and bodies were being found in the adjoining woods.

People were on their guard and near the small town of Bedburg a large wolf was spotted prowling around a nearby creek. The townsfolk armed themselves with slings and spears. They pursued the wolf and just as they were about to attack it they got the shock of their lives. The wolf stood up and it turned out to be a man covered in a wolf's hide.

It was a middle-aged man called Peter Stubbe, who was well known in the area. He was put to torture and revealed a shocking catalogue of crimes. It is best not to go into too much detail but he eventually admitted to killing at least 16 people. He had tried to summon the devil as a twelve-year-old and since then had built some pretty way out fantasies in his head. Eventually the fantasies took over and he began to roam the countryside, attacking people and sucking their blood. He began to eat them. At first he wore a 'wolf's girdle', which was a belt made up of wolf skin, but eventually he wore a whole skin.

Stubbe's family was not safe and he even admitted to eating his young son's brain after cracking his head open with a club.

Stubbe paid for his lycanthropy. He was tortured, beheaded and had his limbs chopped up and suspended on a wheel. On top of the wheel was placed a wolf's head and around its rim hung sixteen bits of wood, each representing one of the souls he had taken. Pretty gruesome.

HOW TO BECOME A WEREWOLF

I wouldn't particularly want to be a werewolf. The idea of running around almost naked on a cold moonlit night doesn't have much appeal. The idea of sniffing other dog's butts has even less appeal.

Despite this, in the past a lot of people have liked the idea of shape-shifting and there were several ways you could become a lycanthrope.

1. Tick off a witch. If you did something to anger a witch she could place an evil curse upon you. She would have to really angry because once a person became a werewolf all of his descendants carried the same hairy genes.

2. Be bitten. The most common way to change was to be bitten or scratched. As soon as the werewolf germ got into your bloodstream you were infected for life.

3. Enter into a pact with the devil. Being a werewolf was kind of like having super powers. You could see in the dark, smell things from miles away, run like the wind and leap huge distances. You also had a taste for very rare meat without needing condiments like mustard or barbecue sauce! By selling your soul to the devil it was possible to be given shape-shifting powers.

4. Putting on a fox skin or girdle. From the very dawn of time humans have tried to gain the strength of animals by wearing their skins. Just think of Native Americans, who wore eagle feathers or bison skins to make themselves fierce warriors. Cave paintings from more than 30,000 years ago show pictures of shamans putting on cave bear skins so that they could inherit the cave bear's strength. A strip of skin wrapped around the waist or a whole skin placed over the head was believed to give the wearer the superhuman strength and cunning of a wolf. This method often involved magical rituals such as dancing around a fire.

5. Magic potion or ointment. Many concoctions could be rubbed over the body to allow a magical transformation. These included

pig or human fat, lard, deadly nightshade and belladonna. Magic mushrooms or henbane could be eaten and these led to hallucinations and black outs.

Never insult a witch!

6. Superstitions. Sometimes you could become a werewolf almost out of bad luck. These causes included: being born on a Friday when there was a full moon, being the seventh child, drinking water from the footprint of a wolf and sleeping outdoors with the full moon shining on your face.

To scare off a werewolf you can cover yourself with the plant called wolfsbane. To make it revert back to a human you must stab him three times in the head with a knife or get three drops of his blood to fall on the ground. To kill a werewolf – fire a silver bullet into its heart!

CHAPTER 6

CURSES AND WITCHCRAFT

TO CURSE OR NOT TO CURSE?
THAT IS THE QUESTION

Curses, magic and witchcraft have been around for as long as humans first became conscious. Neanderthals were engaging in elaborate rituals thousands of years ago. The best preserved European, Otzi the Iceman, had tattoos on his joints. These were no doubt part of some ritual designed to ease arthritic pain and they date back more than 4,000 years ago.

Snake oil salesmen have been around for a long time.

Many ancient rituals were designed to do good. They could guarantee a good hunt or bring rain to water early crops.

But there were also plenty of ancient spells designed to bring as much pain and suffering to people as possible. These types of spells can be termed curses!

Throughout the past many cultures have believed in curses and spells that bring people undone.

POINTING THE BONE

The oldest surviving culture in the world is the Aboriginal Australian culture. Modern DNA studies seem to support the idea that Aboriginals were in the first pulse of modern humans out of Africa, more than 70,000 years ago. On their way through Europe and Asia they interbred with many other human races including the Neanderthal and the mysterious Denisovans. They moved right through South East Asia until about 50,000 years ago, when they reached Australia. Living undisturbed for tens of millennia, the Aboriginals practiced magical rituals that they passed down through the generations.

The Aboriginals had a mystical relationship with the land and there are stories of them being able to communicate with other tribal members even though they were separated by thousands of miles of wilderness. Each tree, rock or billabong had its own spirit, which had to be respected by these hunter gatherers.

If an Aboriginal died from some unexplained cause, their tribe often thought it was due to an evil spirit or spell. They would get revenge on somebody suspected of casting a death spell by Pointing the Bone at the suspected killer. The top men in the tribe would get together and weave a complex series of spells which could drop their target even if he was hundreds of kilometres away.

No doubt you have read the first book in this series, called *A Young Person's Guide to Disgusting Diseases*. This book talks about the placebo effect. This is what happens when somebody who is ill takes a harmless sugar pill but, because they think it has medicine in it, it immediately starts to make them feel better. This is because the patient believes it will do good, so it does do good. Medical tests in fact prove that there is often an improvement – blood pressure can drop, along with cholesterol and all of those nasty modern conditions.

For a curse to work it must have the opposite effect. The cursed person must *believe* that they will get sick or have bad luck for it to take effect.

The best example of this is no doubt the Aboriginal Australian practice of 'singing' or 'pointing the bone'. Once an Aboriginal tribe member believes they are being sung, they can totally give up on life. They stop eating and drinking and waste away. Those are the fortunate ones. Some are so dreadfully petrified with fear that they actually die of fright.

Only one thing could save them: a medicine man from the tribe could 'sing' the end of the spell and tell the poor affected man that the spell was cancelled.

Some tribes from Victoria believed in a magic killer stone. This had a deadly spell put on it before being placed within a pile of the target's poo!

ANCIENT WITCHCRAFT

You might think of the Ancient Greeks as rational and clear thinkers. Not so. They were more superstitious than a bucket load of gypsies.

We have one description of an ancient witch's lair in the book *The Golden Ass*. It was written almost 2,000 years ago and has some pretty gruesome bits. The main character describes all of the tools the witch had at her disposal. She had all kinds of aromatic incense, metal plates engraved with secret signs, beaks and claws of black crows and ravens and bits of human corpse flesh.

In one place she had arranged the noses and fingers of crucified men. In others she had collected the nails that had been driven through palms and ankles. They still had bits of dried flesh sticking to them. She had a collection of skulls of those who had been thrown to wild animals in the amphitheatre as well as little jars full of the blood of men she had murdered. Pamphele, for that was the name of the witch, possessed a large cauldron that she used to concoct her spells. Rotting animal guts were mixed with small tokens from those she sought to curse. Fingernails and hair and even ones or twos could be used for the evil witch to gain power over her victim.

Witches would go to any length to get magical ingredients.

FASCINATING FACTS
VOODOO DOLLS
. . . .

There's a famous comedy sketch where a resistance fighter asks 'What have the Romans ever done for us?'

His Jewish comrades go on to say that the Romans brought peace, roads, water, education, law and order, anchovies, gladiators and a whole lot of other good stuff.

Romans also bought voodoo dolls to their conquered lands! They called them curse dolls.

These weren't some clumsy little fluffy cloth dolls that look like spooky gingerbread men; they were clay models that seemed to scream out pain. Each *curse doll* had its hands and feet tied behind its body and there were small holes in the eyes, mouth, nose, chest, back, head and bum so that iron pins could be stuck right up into them. That wasn't all – often the models had reversed feet or a head twisted right around which showed that all of their internal bones had been broken. Some had their hands or feet chopped off.

The curser had his way with the little clay dolls and inscribed the name of the victim into the clay. To finish the job, the figure would be placed inside a tight fitting box so that no air or light could get in. The box was then thrown into graves or rivers or even into sewers so that the curse would be covered in dirt and filth.

Talk about being unfriended!

The Romans believed that the only way to remove the curse was to find the doll and gradually remove each iron pin. Many sufferers swore to Jupiter that as each pin was removed a lovely feeling of peace settled over them. I suppose that is why so many were buried or tossed into the sea – hard to recover.

The voodoo dolls that were bought into the Caribbean by African slaves seem harmless in comparison. Despite the scary nature of modern day voodoo dolls, they are often used as love charms or for healing magic. Different coloured dolls are often meant to be good for your health.

It is only when a voodoo witch makes a black doll and ties a lock of your hair onto its head or pastes a photo of your face onto the figure that you had better look out.

Romans tossed curses around like confetti.

CURSE TABLETS

The Romans left ruins all over Europe. Great amphitheatres and aqueducts show how grand their empire was. But they also left things called curse tablets that show how petty they were. Curse tablets are little squares of lead. On them are written curses directed at people. Some are quite amusing. Lucullus wrote 'May the scum who stole my sandals from the baths on Tuesday have no rest till they are returned to me.' Others are pretty darn dire: 'I pray to you Jupiter bind her mind so that only gibberish comes from her foul mouth. Liquefy her insides so that postulant corruption leaks from everywhere ...'

Some tablets were used for gambling. Chariot racing was the most popular sport for the Romans and each person had their favourite colour. Curse tablets were used to hobble the opposition team: 'Bind their running, their power, their soul, their onrush, their speed. Take away their victory, entangle their feet, hobble them – make their ankles as thick as wine barrels.'

Modern day curses.

One person lost their gloves and called down an evil curse on their finder: 'The sheet [of lead] which is given to Mercury, that he exacts vengeance for the gloves which have been lost; that he takes blood and health from the person who has stolen them; that he provide what we ask the god Mercury [...] as quickly as possible for the person who has taken these gloves.'

They must have been awfully nice and toasty warm gloves.

Written in the sentences were magical symbols which we do not know the meaning of.

Curse tablets were left wherever they would do the most harm. Temples and sacred springs were popular. Some coffins have tablets that the grudge holder must have slipped in just before the dead person was buried. I wouldn't want to spend eternity buried with a curse calling on the demons of the underworld to rip out my guts and roast them on a barbecue spit!

Curse tablets were used throughout the Greek and Mediterranean world from 500 BCE to 500 CE.

FASCINATING FACTS
CARRYING THE BRIDE ACROSS THE THRESHOLD

In ancient Scotland there were particularly nasty witches around who loved it when married couples lived in misery. They used to place a curse on the doorstep of a newlywed couple's cottage. This curse would make the bride trip as she crossed the threshold and this would doom the whole family to a lifetime of bad luck.

It was the groom's job to avoid this curse and carry his bride over the threshold into their new home. Hopefully she wasn't too big as he'd be condemned to a lifetime of back pain!

Marriage can be a mixed blessing.

MEDIEVAL WITCHES

Just imagine that you were blamed for everything that went bad in your household. If dad got a flat tyre driving to work or a light bulb blew or Harry the Hamster died, wouldn't it be awful if your family ganged up on you and said you were to blame?

That is what happened to witches in the Middle Ages all of the time. If a fungus attacked a crop, a pig died, a cow fell in a ditch and broke a leg, a lady died in childbirth, somebody had a big wart on their nose, a couple couldn't get pregnant or it rained ten days in a row – all of these things would be blamed on witches.

These witches aren't what you see in the movies, all-powerful shape-shifting beings that can turn a man into a mouse. Usually the village 'witch' was a funny old lady who couldn't keep herself clean. Or else it could be that 'man who talks to himself on a train' kind of guy. Anybody who didn't fit in could be branded a witch, even if they had never done anything witchy in their entire life.

Beware of people who talk loudly on trains.

Other people might be branded a witch if they were into folk medicine. I'm sure you know that chicken soup is good for you and no doubt your mum or grandma has recommended some to you. Well lots of other herbs are good for your health and most villages had a herbalist who could make medicines out of natural ingredients. Doctors were rare and very expensive (and they would probably kill you) so villagers often had to ask the medicine lady. In times of trouble the medicine lady could be branded a witch.

WITCH'S SPELLS

Most people accused of being witches weren't, but there were some men and women who did try and MAKE A PACT WITH THE DEVIL so they could CAST DIABOLICAL SPELLS ON THEIR NEIGHBOURS that made their EYES POP OUT and their GIZZARDS MELT LIKE TOFFEE.

One of the most common spells was making a model of somebody out of wax and straw. These dolls could be burned or pricked. One very effective spell was to write a curse on a bit of paper, wrap the doll in the paper and chuck the whole lot in a cess pit.

If there was somebody the witch really wanted to punish she'd get fingernail clippings and hair from the victim. These would then be boiled up with animal guts, pig poo, live toads and urine to make a filthy and sticky mix. The whole lot would be buried in a dung heap and hopefully the nauseous mess caused the victim bad luck.

We think of weddings as happy times. But if a witch got hold of some bridal lace, they could tie a knot in it before burning it and that would make sure the married couple could not have any babies.

Cats were seen as magical animals and were often used in spells. Some English witches tried to kill Queen Anne of Scotland (1665–1714). They found a cat and called it Queen Anne. Then they hacked bits and pieces off a dead man, tied them to the cat, put the cat in a sack and threw the whole lot into the ocean. Apparently this started a frightful storm, which almost sank Queen Anne's ship as she returned from Holland.

CURES TO WITCH'S SPELLS

There were lots of ways to cancel out a witch's spells and the most common one was to kill the witch! If the subject of the spell didn't want to do that, he or she could burn the thatch of her cottage, scratch her bum so the magic leaked out, make her touch the victim or else just ask her to stop.

Some witches got a dose of their own medicine.

If the subject couldn't actually track down the witch, there were some other popular remedies. He could hold pig poo in one hand at the same time as he had a tankard of beer with sage mixed in. Or else he could cut off his hair and chuck it in a fire. Or he could boil his urine in a big copper pot. This last remedy had a positive side effect. Not only did it cancel out the spell but it also stopped the witch from being able to pee.

If the subject really wanted to get down and dirty they could make up a witch bottle. To do this he had to mix his hair, fingernails, some cloth from his clothes and some stale urine in a bottle. This was all then boiled up and it was guaranteed to bring the witch to the victim's door.

Witches gained power over somebody by getting body parts and using them in spells. Mums and dads made sure to burn the bits after they trimmed their children's nails or cut their hair, so that witches could not get their children under their power.

DID YOU KNOW – WITCH TOWERS

In the 15th and 16th Centuries there was a whole lot of hysteria about witches and hundreds of thousands were punished. Any decent sized town built a witch tower (Hexenturm in German) to keep their witches in. It was thought that once a witch was locked up they lost their power because the devil would abandon them. Salzburg in Austria went one step further; they built large copper kettles in their Hexenturm and popped their witches in these as they thought this metal cancelled any magic.

In Bamberg, Germany they went even further. Around 1600 they built the Drudenhaus, which came complete with torture chambers, 26 cells and a courtroom. In one year more than one hundred witches were caught, tried and burnt. The Drudenhaus had a full time torturer and he used thumbscrews, kneescrews, the rack and hot branding irons to make the witches confess. Some 1,500 people died in this way, but not because they were witches. Laws at the time said that the people who caught the witches could keep their houses and money.

WITCH PRICKERS

There was a lot of money to be made by identifying witches. Just by seeing a wrinkly, hairy, hunched, smelly and toothless old hag who dribbled a lot and spoke to herself, any witch hunter could point the finger and say 'there's a witch.' But of course, old ladies like that didn't have much money. It was better to pick on somebody who had a bit of cash.

Now we have pretty much equal rights but back then any woman who argued with her neighbour or who got a bit crotchety could get in big trouble. She could get a scold's bridle put on for a week or so, or she could be accused of being a witch.

Women were treated unfairly in medieval times.

Once someone was accused of being a witch, there were lots tests to prove that they were. The one we all know was to dunk her in water; if she floated she was guilty, if she sank she was innocent. Innocent and usually dead. Another test was for a priest to bless some bread and butter. It was then given to the suspect. If she vomited it up she was a witch.

Many women were stripped naked and professional witch hunters, called witch prickers, checked them all over for the 'Devil's Mark'. This mark could look like a pimple, a sore or a wart, so obviously most women were 'proven' to be witches. The final proof was to prick the Devil's Mark. If it didn't bleed, it was definitely the work of the Dark Lord and proof that she had sold her soul to the Devil.

Many witch prickers had a purpose built knife for this function. It had a retractable point so they could plunge the device in with great fanfare before withdrawing it to reveal no blood or wound. The retractable blade was forced into the handle and a spring would ensure that it emerged as the blade was withdrawn.

Witch prickers made a fortune – by burning innocent people.

The witch was then put on trial. These were the unfairest in history and rules stated that if the suspect said she was innocent it was proof that she was a witch!

A lot of innocent people died after trial. Most were burnt at the stake. But maybe, just maybe, some real witches were burnt too.

CHAPTER 7

LURKING IN THE SHADOWS

If I was walking in a remote wilderness and came face to face with a ten-foot-tall hairy hominid, who walks upright on two feet, my instinct would be to run away at a million miles per hour. Fortunately, it is more likely that the creature would turn and run first. It seems the animals we call Bigfoot are more scared of us than we are of them. With good reason. *Homo sapiens* have managed to destroy most of the megafauna that once walked the earth.

It seems we are not alone. Throughout the world stories abound of wild and woolly critters that move about mysteriously and only occasionally let us humans get a glimpse of them. Some are big and some are small but they have lots of things in common.

Megafauna has good reason to be scared of humans.

All of the animals are bipedal (walk on two legs). So they are all classified as 'crypto-hominids', which can be roughly translated as 'mysterious creatures that walk on two legs'. They are hairy, they make funny 'whoop whoop' noises at night, they seem to be more frightened of us than we are of them, they live in wilderness areas and they all stink! Not just a bad smell like dog breath, but a rancid smell that can often be detected hundreds of metres away. The smell is so strong it often hangs around for quite a while after the animal has run away. That's the other thing all of these weird and wonderful creatures have in common: as soon as they see a human most bolt at a hundred miles an hour, even if they were only discovered by a girl guide in pigtails selling cookies!

Some of the best known critters are:

YOWIE

Most Australians probably don't believe in yowies, but those who have encountered them have no doubt that Australia has its own version of Bigfoot. Maybe most people aren't too convinced because most of the reports of sightings come from grizzled old folk who've spent most of their time wandering the bush doing strange bush stuff. They are often a bit scruffy and are similar to that man on the tram who always has a conversation with himself and pongs a bit like old shoes left out in the rain. The one you don't want to make eye contact with just in case he starts talking to you.

Actually, I'm being a bit unkind. Many yowie sightings are made by regular people just like you and me.

Anyway, all those people who have seen a yowie have no doubt what they have seen and become instant believers. Remarkably, all of the sightings are very similar, whether they are made in the deep wilds of Australia's southern-most state, Tasmania, or the northern-most state of Queensland. This would indicate to me that the yowies have roamed the continent of Australia for perhaps millions of years and called it their home well before the Aboriginals arrived around 50,000 years ago.

YOWIE SPOTTING GUIDE

- They are all seven to nine feet tall.
- They're covered with almost-black shaggy coats that often cover the hands, feet and even the face.
- None have a neck and their broad faces have deep set eyes that glow red at night.
- They are upright, very mobile and usually retreat when seen. Their arms are so long that they extend to well below the knees.
- They are adept at using sticks and stones as tools, and are omnivorous.
- All yowies are sited near wilderness areas. Some are seen on the edges. Others are discovered deep in many of Australia's national parks when bushwalkers stumble across them.
- They stink.

The most remarkable thing about yowies is definitely their smell. Other bipedal-megafauna do tend to stink a bit, but their Australian cousins smell so bad that many who encounter the beasts are not sure whether to run away or vomit! I'm not sure if you've ever had the experience of coming across a dead animal. All of a sudden, when you get close, there is an awful, awful stench.

DEEP SET EYES
(THAT GLOW RED!)

BROAD
FACE

NO NECK

THEY
STINK!

7 TO 9 FEET TALL!

HAIR
EVERYWHERE!

SUPER
LONG
ARMS

USE STICKS AND
STONES AS TOOLS

111

As you pass that smell hangs around in your nostrils for a bit, even though the smell is no longer there.

Well, with yowies the smell often arrives well before the yowie is sighted or even heard! Here is a story from two people who had a close encounter.

Don't get between a yowie and his tucker.

Two Queenslanders were camped in the depths of a National Park in New South Wales. They had a beautiful spot looking over a deep billabong. They were enjoying the solitude that only a walk well away from tracks and towns can bring.

As the two prepared to settle in for the evening and enjoy a cup of tea, a strange smell wafted towards them. The two campers looked at each other with dismay. Things got even worse when a huge hairy man appeared on the other side of the billabong and let out an almighty roar. The animal seemed to be enraged and seized a huge branch, which it snapped in two as if it was a match stick. One of the men grabbed a rifle and let off a shot at the beast. The bullet didn't hit but the loud noise had the desired effect and the amazing creature disappeared into the bush. The two men could still hear the enraged bellows as the animal fled.

The Queenslanders built the biggest fire possible and spent most of the night feeling pretty darn nervous. With good reason. The branch that the creature had snapped was at least 20cm thick! The last thing they wanted was a midnight visit.

The following morning the campers went around the billabong to where they had seen the yowie. They found several huge footprints and caught a slight whiff of the disgusting smell.

They camped for one or two more days. Just before they were about to leave, an interesting discovery was made. Just behind their campsite was an abandoned old farmhouse. Nothing remained except for a brick fire place. There was also an old potato field, which was still producing quite a crop even though it had been abandoned years ago. There were quite deep holes everywhere. Some were freshly turned. The two men worked out that the yowie was so angry because he thought the two interlopers were trying to take his potatoes!

ABOMINABLE SNOWMAN AND BIGFOOT

No doubt the best known two-legged ape-like giant is the abominable snowman, which is regularly sighted in the Himalayas. Its close cousin is Bigfoot, who is found in America. All of these animals are over ten feet tall, have huge feet and long powerful arms and are entirely covered in fur. Bigfoot (otherwise known as a sasquatch) has deep brown or even black fur, while the abominable snowman (also known as the yeti) is white. No doubt the yeti is white to blend in with the snow covered terrain of the Himalayas. Bigfoot is most commonly encountered in the warmer forests of the west coast of America and is much darker so it can hide under the dense forest.

Apart from the colour of the hair it seems the animals are pretty much identical. They have a pronounced brow ridge as well as crest of bone on top of their heads. Their eyes are dark. Both have an upturned nose like a gorilla's and solid gorilla jawbones that lack thick lips. The yeti usually has hair covering his cheekbones, while Bigfoot has a more gorilla-like naked face.

Bigfoot is the most famous crypto-hominid, probably because of the hundreds of tall stories told about this tall animal. It can be quite aggressive, as the following stories show.

The name Bigfoot comes from encounter that a man called Jerry Crew had while working in the woods of Northern California. He was a tractor operator on a road site. The first inkling he and his fellow workers had that something was not quite right was when a huge tractor tyre was thrown into a nearby gully. In the morning the men awoke to find huge footprints pressed into the mud all around their campsite. He took some plaster casts of the prints to the local newspaper and a headline screamed 'Bigfoot', which was then adopted as the most common name for the creature.

It's possible that the Bigfoot found in the previous story didn't like intruders in their territory. All primates are territorial and there is no reason to think that a ten-foot muscle-bound monster with huge teeth and an offensive smell wouldn't feel the same!

In 1892 a trapper called Bauman and his partner were setting traps in the wilderness of Montana's Wisdom River. When they returned to their camp they found their tent and camping equipment trashed by some large animal. At night things got worse when they heard a huge beast bashing its way through the trees. The two men were terrified and in the morning abandoned their camp. They separated and Bauman went to check the traps while his partner set off downriver to set up camp.

When Bauman got to the new site he was horrified to find his friend lying with his neck snapped and huge tooth marks up and down his throat. The trapper fled as fast as he could and never returned to the campsite to retrieve his skins or bury his friend!

Albert Ostman had a very close encounter – he was kidnapped by a family of sasquatches. While camping in the remote forest of British Columbia in 1924, he woke to find that someone or something had picked up his sleeping bag like a sack and carried him off. After much bouncing and banging he was released from the bag. Peering out of the opening Ostman saw that he was surrounded by a sasquatch nuclear family! It was complete with mummy sasquatch, daddy sasquatch and two little kiddie sasquatches. Even though they were kids, the young ones were four and six feet high. The family went about its daily business of gathering food while communicating with grunts, clicks and even hand signals. Although they never hurt the lumberjack, they made sure he could not leave.

Ostman finally escaped. He had managed to retain a snuff box and when the male sasquatch saw him snifftering it up his nose he too wanted a go. A flat sasquatch nose can take in a lot more snuff than our puny noses, and the poor beast fell back, bellowing in pain. Ostman saw his chance and did a runner, not stopping until he came across a friendly logging camp. He didn't tell his tale until thirty years later in the fear that he would be ridiculed.

Come and meet the new neighbours.

SKUNK APE

Florida residents don't only have to worry about alligators, snakes and skunks. Hidden deep in the swampy wetlands that cover much of the territory is the skunk ape. It has many other names, including the swamp cabbage man, Florida Bigfoot, swampsquatch, Florida sandman and the stink ape.

The skunk ape.

All of the mysterious hominids are said to be very smelly, but given that Florida swamps are some of the hottest and most humid places on earth it is likely that these mysterious creatures are particularly rank. Some of the sightings report the creature to be up to ten feet tall, but most place it in the range of five to six feet. All agree that the animal is covered in matted dark fur and has long arms. Uniquely though, some say there is a tail on these animals. It is likely that the skunk ape is an omnivore, as it has been observed stealing fruit from backyard orchards as well as killing chickens and livestock. One possible food source is the rotten leavings of alligator kills, which would account for the disgusting smell.

Florida's everglades are steamy, jungle-like environments and it is easy for the stink ape to disappear once sighted. Some close sightings, including photos, could place the animal in the orang-utan family.

MAWAS

These ten-foot-high animals are exactly like Bigfoot except they are commonly reported in the Johor jungles of Malaysia. They too are covered with dark fur, except for on their palms and faces. They have a prominent brow ridge, an upturned nose and thick lips. They are also found in the Philippines, where the locals call it the Muwa. These animals are rarely seen but are often heard calling out at night. The calls are like the squeals of wild pigs ending in a rough cough like a gibbon. They are also heard crashing through underbrush as they flee any human contact.

Some of the best evidence to prove the existence of the Mawas are numerous huge footprints found on creek shores or on dirt roads.

Another name is hantu jarang gigi, which translates as 'snaggle toothed ghosts'. I've got no idea why!

Europeans first recorded eight sightings of the gigantic bipeds as long ago as 1871.

ORANG PENDEK

Not much wilderness remains on earth, but on the island of Sumatra (the sixth largest island in the world) there are still vast tracts of inaccessible and unexplored rainforest. It seems that here lives an unknown hominid: the Orang Pendek. There have been thousands of sightings of this mysterious creature. It is upright and walks on two short legs, has incredibly wide, square shoulders and is covered in hair that is described as either mud coloured or red. It has long arms but walks remarkably like a human according to eyewitnesses, who have seen it disappear when spotted. Hairs, footprints and handprints from the creature have been found and scientists agree they are from no known species.

It is possible that the Orang Pendek is related to orang-utans. There was an ancient race of apes called *Sivapithecus* that lived 12.5 million years ago. Their bodies were like modern day chimps but they had heads similar to modern day orang-utans. This ancient ape lineage split into modern day orang-utans as well as the giant *Gigantopithecus blacki*. The orang-utan split into two lineages which still live today. One is strong and muscular but is more ape-like when it walks, while the other is slimmer and more upright. Both species live in different areas in Borneo and Sumatra. It is possible that a third type evolved, a ground dwelling orang-utan that forages below the trees rather than in them.

Perhaps the Orang Pendek is a surviving member of the *Gigantopithecus blacki* which has shrunk. This happens to many animals that are cut off on islands when seas rise. Since there is less land to gather food on, animals stuck on islands must shrink to survive.

YEREN

The Yeren is a Chinese wild man and there have been four hundred sightings in recent years. They seem to be mainly concentrated in the mountainous Hubei province. Many comment on the animal's human-like eyes. They seem to be able to convey emotions just like ours, although they rest of the face is more ape-like. Yeren usually have reddish brown, long fur similar to an orang-utan.

Long hair is always an advantage in the mountains.

They have large bottoms and bellies and take off pretty quickly if spotted. It seems that they are pretty similar to the Orang Pendek, although they live in a colder climate. For this reason their hair is a lot longer. A rare few are reported as having white hair. No doubt this is an evolutionary alteration to allow them to hide during the winter months.

LIKELY SUSPECTS

Gigantopithecus blacki is definitely my favourite as a possible explanation for the yeti. This crazy critter was a giant ape that first split from our genetic line approximately 15 million years ago and evolved into the largest ape ever six million years later. Its remains have been found all around Asia. It stood up to ten feet (three metres) tall and was three times heavier than most modern men, weighing in at a massive 270 kilograms. Studies of the creature's tooth enamel indicate that it was a vegetarian and mainly ate foods found in forests. It lived for millions of years in many areas, including Northern China, so could easily have made its way across the Bering Strait into America during one of the many Ice Ages that allowed other creatures, including man, to cross over to the new continent. Gigantopithecus remains have been found as far south as Vietnam so it could easily have got a bit further south where it is now known as Mawas or Orang Pendek.

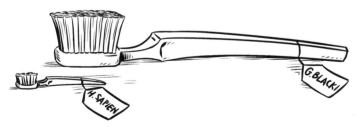

METRES

3

2

1

G. BLACKI   H. SAPIEN   P. PYGMAEUS
                  (HUMAN)   (ORANGUTAN)

But the real reason I think *Gigantopithecus blacki* is such a good candidate for so many of the upright mystery men is the fossil record – actually, the lack of fossil records. Only teeth and a few jawbones have been found (Chinese herbalists used to grind up the teeth and sell them as 'dragon dust') so it is really hard to know exactly what it looked like. The teeth seem similar to an orang-utans. It may have loped along on all fours like a gorilla, or more likely it looked more like an orang-utan. *Gigantopithecus blacki* could have even evolved to stand upright.

Two other fossils support the idea that this animal could be our modern day yeti. Fossilised teeth found in India show that one subspecies was a lot smaller than its larger cousins, not much larger than a modern day chimp. This could account for the different sizes around the world.

Secondly, a tooth found in a Thailand cave was surrounded by the remains of lots of other animals. Some of these animals were plains dwellers that ate grass, and others were forest dwellers. So *Gigantopithecus blacki* lived in forest intermixed with plains, just like many of the locations where yetis are found today.

Finally, there is nothing in the archaeological record to say why our very distant cousin went extinct. Maybe it didn't.

Who's to say that this fantastic great ape didn't evolve into many subspecies that are still alive today?

EBU GOGO

The people living on the island of Flores in the Indonesian archipelago have many stories of a crypto-hominid. They call this mystical being Ebu gogo, which roughly translates as 'little wrinkled one who eats anything'.

These animals were like little people and were half as high as adult humans. They lived in caves deep in the Flores jungles, were covered in hair and had flat noses. Their faces were wide but they were short and would only come up to the waist of adults. Ebu gogo could run very fast. They are described as about a metre tall, with long hair, pot bellies, ears that slightly stick out, a slightly awkward gait, and longish arms and fingers. They could climb slender trees but spent most of their time on the ground.

Often at night the villagers living in their bamboo huts heard the little people scurrying around looking for food. They spoke in a funny language that included whistles, clicks and low mumbled words. Some came close to the villagers and could mimic any words or even sentences that they heard. If a villager said 'take this food' the Ebu gogo would repeat 'take this food' before scurrying off. Ebu gogo would eat anything that was raw, including vegetables, fruit, grains and meat. Some became so common that plates of food were left out at night. The plates were made of pumpkin and even they were devoured.

The villagers who entertained Ebu gogo came to regret their kindness – the hairy little visitors got a taste for human meat and would sneak in at night to steal babies before running off and devouring them. This was too much and hunting parties were sent out to chase off the unwelcome visitors. Some were killed while others were smoked out of their caves and forced to flee. The women Ebu gogo had extremely pendulous breasts, so long that they would throw them over their shoulders when they had to run.

The last Ebu gogo were seen heading to the west of the island towards a mountain range. Within this mountain range was a huge cave called Liang Bua.

Not all of our bipedal cousins were friendly.

This is not the only story of what happened to the fierce little hominids. Believe it or not, even today some villagers on the 24-mile-long island can imitate the little people's way of talking as if they heard them just yesterday. Some villagers say the 'animals' were very common until the Portuguese and Dutch settlers began to arrive in the 17th Century. Others say they are still to be found in the remaining stands of forest.

These are great stories, but unlike other crypto-hominids there is proof that these Ebu gogo actually existed. We call them hobbits and the scientists call them *Homo floresiensis* (Flores man).

And what is more amazing is it seems that these little people emerged from Africa more than two million years ago and are related to one of our earliest ancestors, *Homo habilis* (handy man).

This means that you should get every book you can find about our ancestors, whether they are in the school library or at home, and BURN THEM because they are ALL WRONG. Any book written before this one will say that *Homo erectus* (don't laugh) was the first hominid to move out of Africa. They were just like modern humans but had a smaller brain case.

It used to be believed that *Homo erectus* moved through Europe and into Asia more than one million years ago. The theory goes on that some *Homo erectus* evolved into Neanderthals while others evolved into modern *Homo sapiens* (thinking man, i.e. us – doesn't apply to your younger brother). The theory continues that about 100 thousand years ago *Homo sapiens* spread out from Africa, wiping out anything in its way.

When hobbits were first dug up from that cave Liang Bua in 2003, by New Zealander Mike Morwood, the archaeologists around the world tried to fit them into the existing ideas. Some scientists thought they were a race of people who suffered a rare brain shrinking disease (encephalopathy). Others thought it was a type of *Homo erectus* who had shrunk.

The age old question: who is going to eat who?

It now seems that the little *Homo habilis* left Africa at least a million years earlier than *Homo erectus* and set out across the world colonising continents and islands. And they were not primitive, stupid little half monkeys. They had to cross at least 25km of open sea to get to Flores. Once they were there they found a land occupied by giant storks, dwarf elephant-like creatures (*Stegodon*) and rats the size of dogs! Even worse, the bloodthirsty giant Komodo dragon would have loved snacking on the little hairy people.

Morwood also found stone tools on neighbouring Sulawesi that dated to two million years ago. The Ebu gogo had a huge range of sophisticated tools and weapons. They used fire to cook their meat. What is pretty amazing is the fact that they would have had to use complex hunting techniques to fight and kill the dangerous animals living on Flores. It is possible that our earliest ancestors lived just to the north of Australia for two million years! This has been supported by recent finds that prove the hominid before *Homo habilis – Australopithecus –* was using stone tools to butcher animals up to four million years ago!

If scientists got this theory so badly wrong, who's to say all of the other creatures we have talked about in this chapter don't exist? The bones of Flores man fit *exactly* with the islanders' descriptions of Ebu gogo. Some scientists think that maybe the little creatures evolved from *Homo erectus*. Wherever they came from, they were amazingly brave little creatures.

CHAPTER 8

MONSTERS FROM THE DEPTHS OF TIME

Australian monsters are real. Huge clawed beasts grab little children and take them down to the depths of the deepest billabong. Carnivores with razor sharp teeth drop from trees, pouncing onto the unwary and ripping their throats out. Dragons longer than a classroom can kill the largest animal with just one bite.

All of these animals are real. Thousands of fossilised remains have been unearthed all around Australia. Aboriginal myths describe their behaviours in great detail. European stories show that they may have encountered them less than 100 years ago. Chances are that many of these magnificent and mysterious marsupials still inhabit remote regions of Australia, just waiting to pounce on and eat any bushwalker who is unlucky enough to cross their path. Some of their relatives still live in islands just to the north of Australia.

FASCINATING FACTS
CARNIVORE VEGETARIANS
. . . .

Whenever a lion or some such carnivore brings down a herbivore like a wildebeest or bison, the first thing they eat is the guts. Inside the guts are lots and lots of half-digested greens such as grass and leaves. Once they've eaten their veg, they get stuck into the meaty bits. So in fact carnivores have a balanced diet! Don't ask me about vampires though – I'm not sure how a meal of pure blood can be considered balanced.

Even carnivores need a balanced diet.

THE DROP BEAR

Nowadays many people laugh when they are told the story of the drop bear. Wise guy tour guides try to get their bushwalking charges scared with ridiculous stories about catastrophically cruel carnivorous koalas. Rather than being cute and cuddly, these arboreal predators are armed with razor sharp talons at the end of their little koala paws. Instead of having short, stubby teeth, these killer koalas have long, curved fangs, which they use to rip open the throat of their hapless prey. One sub-species, say these guides, actually prefer to tear out the eyeballs of their victims.

But all of these killers have one thing in common: they are ambush predators who drop from trees onto their prey and rip them to shreds before getting stuck into their guts and gooey bits.

These stories are not made up.

They are true.

Carnivorous koala.

But instead of talking about carnivorous koalas they are really talking about *Thylacoleo carnifex* – the marsupial lion.

This creature is the stuff of nightmares. It is about the size of a leopard or a very, very large dog. Rather than being streamlined for quick movement, the *Thylacoleo carnifex* is a bundle of huge leg, shoulder, neck and jaw muscles that are as tough and taut as iron. Nevertheless, they could run pretty fast. If you had a dodgy leg, you'd be hunted down quick smart.

If this animal dropped on you it would be like being hit by a minibus; a minibus with four huge fangs! Behind the front fangs were not a set of teeth like you might expect. All the teeth morphed into insanely sharp long tooth-blades that snapped together like a pair of scissors. One bite of the mighty jaws could separate your head from your shoulder as easily as you might bite down on a banana. In fact scientists have proved that the huge neck and jaw muscles gave the marsupial lion the STRONGEST BITE OF ANY MAMMALIAN OR MARSUPIAL ANIMAL IN HISTORY.

Saber-tooth tigers, cave lions, tigers – they've got nothing on *Thylacoleo carnifex*. This jaw could only move up or down, without any sideways motion. It must have torn off chunks of meat before raising its mouth to the air and gulping down. In front of these teeth were incisors that projected forward like a lion's fangs.

The marsupial lion: a gold medal bone breaker.

This killer had as its prey wombats the size of a pickup truck, birds higher than a basketball ring and kangaroos that could look into a second-storey window.

The *Thylacoleo carnifex* has another weapon in its armoury. Facing inwards from its brick-like front paws were two huge thumb claws, which it used to rip open the stomachs of its prey so that their guts poured out onto the dusty Australian earth. These 6cm long claws were retractable and found on the end of very long and strong arms. Just like your little pussy Moffy or Ginger, they could climb trees and claw the life out of you.

Australian scientists have debated how the *Thylacoleo carnifex* hunted its prey. Its long arms and strong claws indicate it was probably a tree dweller that could run pretty quickly if needed. It may have used its incisors to strangle its prey after it had knocked it to the ground with its solid claw mounted paws. One crazy theory says that the sharp, long blade tooth was used to run up to kangaroos or *Diprotodons* and rip open their pouches. The little baby joeys would tumble down, where they would be gobbled up.

So while you can laugh at the humorous stories of the drop bear, remember: they are all shadows of your worst possible nightmare, the marsupial lion.

THE BUNYIP

Before we begin talking about the bunyip I want to tell you about another animal that early settlers at first didn't believe in. When reports were sent back to England describing the platypus, they were met with disbelief. How could an animal have a flat body shaped like a lizard, fur like a mammal, a bill like a duck and a flat tail like a beaver? Not to mention four paddles for feet, two of which had a sharp spike on them that could inject deadly venom. When the first stuffed specimens got back to England, botanists tried to find joins where all the bits had been sewn together.

Bunyip billabong.

They couldn't find any of course because the platypus was a real animal that had evolved millions and millions of years ago. On a positive note, the platypus used to be a threatened species but now there are lots and lots of them throughout Australia.

You might wonder why I'm talking about the platypus in a chapter on bunyips but it will soon become clear.

Early British settlers who penetrated into uncharted bushland often heard a whoop-whoop noise at the dead of night. Aboriginal guides began to tremble and explained that it was the bunyip making the calls – and the bunyip was angry. The cries echoed up and down gorges and through the gum trees.

The explorers noted one other thing – when the bunyip was calling, every other animal went silent like the grave. Frogs stopped croaking and night birds stopped calling. Even the high pitched chirps made by bats hunting prey stopped altogether. It seemed that the bunyip was king of its domain.

Aboriginal tribes throughout Australia all believed in the bunyip and they all feared it. When Europeans came to Australia they found that Aboriginals were divided into lots of different tribes, often with different languages. In fact, it's been estimated that there were 5,000 different languages spoken. Or is that 500? Oh well, there sure were a lot of languages. The different tribes had different names for the bunyips. Some called them the Banib, the Kurreah or the Mindie. In South Australia it was known as the Muglewongk.

Even though the bunyips were given different names, all Aboriginal people agreed that is was a very dangerous animal. It lived in billabongs (Australian lakes with reeds around the edges) and rivers. It could also be found in large waterholes in creeks. The bunyip was a fierce protector of its territory and any person who came too close could be eaten up and swallowed whole. The bunyip particularly liked little children and if it caught a youngster it would grab the little tyke in its huge claws and drag him down to the bottom of the water. The bunyips were particularly dangerous around summer or spring – the breeding time for most animals.

There were several large water holes along the Euhayli River in New South Wales. It was taboo for locals to visit as they would be dragged underwater and never seen again. Even on the other side of the continent in Western Australia the Noongar people spoke of the Marghrett. This was a strange looking animal with a huge bum and a narrow chest. It would creep up on an unwary tribesperson in the middle of the night, hook its huge claws around their ankles and drag them into the water. Once they were in the water the Marghrett would bite them with its sharp teeth and carry them down into the depths, never to be seen again.

The bunyip did not only have different names. Nobody was quite sure what it looked like.

William Buckley had the most amazing life of anybody I have heard of. Ever.

He was born in Ireland and soon grew to be a six-foot-four giant with pale skin and bright red hair. Buckley joined the British Army and fought against the French in the Napoleonic wars. When discharged the Irishman fell into a life of crime and was transported as a convict to the colonies of Australia. He then joined the ill-fated expedition to begin a settlement in Port Phillip at a place called Sorrento. He escaped from the penal colony there and went all around the bay and into the hills nearby.

Buckley then had a most amazing stroke of luck. After travelling on foot for several weeks he was awfully hungry. The escaped convict came across a burial mound with a spear sticking out of it. The local Aboriginals used to bury their menfolk in a shallow grave but put rocks and dirt on top so the dingoes could not get to the dead bodies. They then stuck the warrior's favourite spear into the mound so he could go hunting in the afterlife.

Now old Buckley did not know any of this, but when he saw the spear he knew he could use it so he pulled it out of the burial mound. He was walking through the bush when suddenly he was surrounded by about twenty Aboriginal warriors, howling and stamping and getting ready to attack the English convict.

You see, Aboriginals used to think that ghosts were very tall and had pale skin and red hair! Then one observant fellow saw the spear that Buckley was holding. 'Stop!' he cried. 'That's our cousin back from the dead – look, he's even carrying his spear.'

So that was it. Buckley was welcomed into the tribe and

137

he lived with them for more than *thirty years* from 1803 to 1835!

During this time the Irishman saw many things, and he actually saw a bunyip.

I could never see any part of it except the back, which appeared to be covered with feathers of a dusky grey colour. It seemed to be about the size of a full-grown calf. When alone I several times tried to spear a Bun-yip: but had the natives seen me do so it would have caused great displeasure. And again had I succeeded in killing or even wounding one my own life would have been over; they consider the animal something supernatural.

Bunyip stories aren't always to be believed.

Lots of settlers and explorers had different kinds of experiences. In 1818 the explorer Hamilton Hume found the skin of a large water dwelling animal while mapping the new colony of New South Wales. Sadly, he didn't keep it, but his description caused such a stir that other expeditions went to the location that Hume mentioned, looking for the watery critter.

One settler had a very creepy bunyip experience near Melrose in South Australia. While preparing to row across a river he noticed a dark shape moving just below the surface of the water. It seemed pretty big and gave the farmer a queer feeling in his stomach. He ducked down among the reeds and watched the shape, until suddenly it broke through the surface with an angry bellow. He described that the creature had a huge head with bristly black hair and a long neck like a horse. Later on in the Melrose pub he told his mates that he reckoned it was up to four metres long.

In the 1890s the Warra Warra waterhole in Queensland was host to lots of sightings of a bunyip. In one month six people saw it, but nobody could agree exactly what they saw.

Some eyewitnesses thought the bunyip was similar to a giant snake that would wrap up its prey like a boa constrictor, and some said it would look around and pant like a dog!

What could the creature be?

Well, just like when the platypus was first described, it was a confusing mess of bits and pieces. When archaeologists first stumbled upon the animal that is probably the bunyip they could not believe what they found. It seemed to be a critter made of lots of bizarre bits stuck together with Blu Tack and super glue (and maybe a post-it note).

Palorchestes azael was a fearsome sight and absolutely unique as far as marsupials go. It seemed to be a cross between a sloth and a wombat, but it had a fearsome array of weapons at its disposal. It was the size of a large horse and had huge arms equipped with razor sharp claws up to 12cm long. It was probably a swamp dweller and perhaps used these claws to gather in large clumps of reeds to eat. And believe it or not, it seems old *Palorchestes azael* didn't have a normal mouth like most marsupials but in fact had a trunk. And not only did it have a trunk, but it seems to have had a huge elongated tongue which could whip out and grab weeds and grasses to stuff them into its maw. Huge ripping canines finished off the armament, along with 10cm-long claws on its back legs.

At first archaeologists thought that it was a species of kangaroo, but as more fossils were found it now appears that the animal might have been a water dweller. They lived alongside Aboriginals until at least 20,000 years ago, but probably a lot longer.

So let's paint a picture of *Palorchestes azael* as the first Aboriginals to get to Australia might have seen it. Lumbering out of the swamp would come an ungainly animal with front arms almost as long as its body. These arms ended with mighty clubbed fists which had sword-like claws almost as long as a human head. In front of the shoulders was a huge long neck and a long head with a trunk sticking out front. On either side of the trunk were large tusk-like teeth. The back of the *Palorchestes azael*'s body was even stranger. It had a huge wide bum and comparatively short and stocky rear legs. It would lumber along on land like a big, uncoordinated teddy bear from hell, and occasionally sit down in front of a tree or fern and use its claws and trunk to strip off foliage and even bark.

But if the *Palorchestes azael* was startled it would lurch in huge ungainly strides to its billabong and leap underwater. Here it was safe, as it could breathe through the tip of its trunk. It would also transform into a streamlined underwater swimmer, with its huge arms able to propel it around in the water at enormous speed. It was transformed into a deadly aquatic killer – especially if you went near its young.

Frankenstein's bunyip.

Everybody thinks of kangaroos as friendly, furry animals that love a pat. But don't go near a bull-kangaroo when it's mating time as they become very, very aggressive and can use their hind legs to eviscerate (rip the guts out of) any animal that comes too close.

Kangaroos aren't always cute and cuddly.

The *Palorchestes azael* was probably pretty similar and I can't imagine anything scarier than one coming at me at a million miles per hour.

There are some interesting facts that aren't that interesting because everybody knows them. Well of course one well known interesting fact is that more people are killed in Africa by angry hippopotamuses (or is that hippopotami?) than any other animal. I reckon the *Palorchestes azael* fulfilled pretty much the same role in the Australian ecosystem. They'd hole up in their watery hides during the day and come out at night to scavenge and feed. But with the slightest swipe of their massive forearm they could transform anybody who came too close into so much yabby bait.

I think *Palorchestes azael* should be renamed *Bunyip magnum et formidulosus*: the big and scary bunyip.

FASCINATING FACTS
THE LARGEST KANGAROO EVER
. . . .

This animal was called the *Procoptodon goliah* and was three metres tall; this would be almost the height of a basketball hoop (10 feet). It weighed three times the average weight of a modern human at 250 to 300 kilograms. Rather than having weak little front arms it had long limbs that it used to reach up into the trees to get leaves.

Family gathering: wallaby meets goliah.

On the end of the front feet were two long fingers with two long claws shaped like grappling hooks that could tear down vegetation. It had a blunt face with forward facing eyes and huge horse-like feet with one long claw that morphed into a hoof. Its tendons and muscles were arranged just like a modern day kangaroo, so it is likely old *Procoptodon goliah* could bound and hop around just like Skippy – just three times higher and three times faster!!!

Like most of the megafauna it became extinct pretty much straight after humans arrived.

Believe it or not, its closest living relative is the banded hare-wallaby, which is probably the cutest little marsupial critter you can ever imagine.

THE NATIVE DRAGON

Perhaps the scariest story told by the Aboriginals involved a giant four legged dragon that used to terrorise a tribe in the forests of North Queensland.

This was a hideous beast: a ten-metre-long (as long as a normal classroom) giant goanna with a thick scaly hide that resisted even the sharpest spears. Its mouth was always drooling with bloody saliva and the huge dragon's breath was so disgusting that it withered shrubs and could make anybody pass out if they got close enough to it.

The dragon would lie in wait in the forest and whenever a little kid walked past it would leap out of cover and grab the child. It then scurried back to its cave, where it would eat the unfortunate boy or girl. Sometimes the dragon got so brave it would come into the tribe's campsite and grab adults.

Death by bad breath.

The tribe's warriors tried to attack the beast but its fearsome armour protected it. What was worse was that if it managed to give a warrior even the tiniest cut with its teeth the warrior would soon sicken and die.

The tribe was being decimated, so they went to the local medicine man and pleaded for help.

'This is what you must do,' said the wise man. 'Go into the jungle and catch as many bright red or yellow tree frogs as you can find. Then hunt a kangaroo. Slit the kangaroo's belly open and place the frogs inside. Sew him up with some reed twine and leave the kangaroo outside the dragon's lair.'

The tribe's warriors did as they were told. At night time the men crept up to the cave and left the kangaroo carcass outside its gloomy entrance.

They waited until the morning and saw the monster's massive snout poke out of the cave. A huge forked tongue snaked out of its mouth and seemed to point at the dead kangaroo. In a frightening burst of speed, the huge lizard sprung upon the corpse and dragged it into its filthy den. The warriors heard the kangaroo's bones being crunched up and a whole lot of slurping and slushing as it devoured its meal.

This turned out to be the last meal enjoyed by the dragon. Soon the warriors heard a mighty bellowing as the poison from the tree frogs entered its system. These little amphibians of course produce one of the most lethal poisons on earth and the lizard thrashed around as the toxins froze its nervous system, leading to paralysis of its lungs and heart. Soon the mighty monitor was no more and the tribe could live in peace.

When the first European settlers heard this story they laughed at it and put it down to the Aboriginals' active imaginations. They had their silly grins wiped off their faces when archaeologists found remains that fit the story perfectly.

The fossilised animal was called *Megalania prisca*, which translates as 'ancient giant butcher'. It was a fearsome animal that apparently pretty much died out about 40,000 years ago. That is the date of the most recent fossils, but of course it may have lived in parts of Australia a lot longer. Some people believe that it still lives in isolated pockets. Its earliest fossils date to about two million years ago.

So for two million years *Megalania prisca* roamed Australia and possibly Papua New Guinea. It was the nastiest, meanest critter ever. It had huge ripping teeth closely lined up on massive jaws. The head was about five feet long! In the jaws just below the gums were sacs that produced venom. It was the largest poisonous animal ever to live and there were grooves along its teeth so that whenever it bit something the victim would be infected by the lethal toxin, which would get into the animal's blood system and slowly kill it. The venom also had anti-clotting agents. This meant that the new wound would never heal but would continue to bleed. Not only that but *Megalania prisca* had even worse breath than Snotty Evans in 7G. They fed on carrion, which is dead rotting meat, and between their teeth were hundreds of lethal bacteria and viruses, which would also infect anything they bit.

'Mmm, no poo there.'

The *Megalania prisca* actually has a living relative, the Komodo dragon, and they probably hunted in pretty much the same manner. The dragons lie in wait along paths or near waterholes, and when an animal approaches they turn on an incredible burst of speed and attack it. They either swipe with their giant claws the leg tendons, bringing down the prey, or they give it an almighty bite with their disease ridden mouth. Even if the animal escapes, the dragon uses its super sensitive long tongue to sniff blood particles in the air and follow the dying animal to its doom. Since it tracked its prey by smell, the giant lizard would have been able to track its wounded prey at day or night and would just lope along for miles and miles until exhaustion and bacteria brought it down. Once the animal tracked down its prey, it was feast time. A Komodo dragon can eat 80% of its body weight in one sitting and our Australian monster could probably do just the same. To make sure it doesn't eat any poo in the lower intestine, it grabs the offending article in its mouth and whizzes it around so all of the poo flies around away from the bits it wants to eat. Try doing that at Christmas dinner in front of Aunty Madge.

Then for a nasty finish to the whole process, the giant reptile would lie down and digest its meal. Once digested it could burp up large balls of indigestible material such as hooves, teeth and claws.

This monster fed on the giant marsupial herbivores for millions of years and no doubt it was the most horrible animal that the Aboriginal Australians had to contend with when they arrived on the continent 50,000 years ago.

Nevertheless, sometimes in the huge forests that still exist in Australia, some witnesses have said they have seen giant lizards prowling in the undergrowth. Also there are regular reports of cows being torn apart and almost completely eaten. These reports are also common in Papua New Guinea.

Sceptics say that it would be impossible to have breeding pairs go undetected. But Komodo dragons and related reptiles can lay eggs by parthenogenesis. This is where one female can lay fertile eggs without the help from the male.

Maybe in an undiscovered waterhole in some secluded part of the Australian outback there is still a remnant population of *Megalania prisca* waiting to leap out and consume an unsuspecting Japanese tourist.

'You call that a talon? THIS is a talon!'

FASCINATING FACTS
RECORD-BREAKING EAGLE
· ·

As everybody who has seen *The Lord of the Rings* trilogy knows, it's an absolute corker of a scene when (WARNING – WARNING – SPOILER ALERT) Frodo finally gets the One Ring into the flames of Mount Doom. Mount Doom blows up, the dark tower collapses and it's on for young and old. But when Frodo and Sam are rescued by the giant eagles, many clever people have a nagging thought. 'Why didn't Gandalf stick Frodo and the Ring on an eagle at the start of Book One and have the whole thing over in a day or so?' Good thinking – but then we would have had a 20 page book and a 15 minute movie!

I decided to bring this up because *The Lord of the Rings* movies were shot in New Zealand, and the largest eagle in history originally came from New Zealand.

When the Māoris first arrived in New Zealand at about 1000 CE they found the islands populated by giant birds. Since no mammals were on the land the birds had evolved into every ecological niche. So some giant birds ate nuts, others ate grass and some ate trees. A lot of these moas were absolutely huge and stood up to four metres tall. The smallest flightless birds were like the kiwi, a species which is still alive.

Anyway, as you are no doubt aware, where there are a whole lot of herbivores (vegetarians) there will always be a carnivore (meat eaters). In New Zealand it was the giant eagle, called Haast's eagle. It had a huge wingspan of three metres wide and its bones indicate it was the heaviest eagle ever, with a total weight of up to 18 kilograms.

Its hunting strategy would have been simple. Moas are basically big birds with a very long neck. The Haast's eagle would descend from the sky and smash its huge beak or talons into the moa's spinal column, just below the head. This New Zealand eagle had a much stronger jaw than modern eagles, but the real kicker were its talons. The front ones were six centimetres long, but the rear one was up to eleven centimetres long.

They had a wide tail, which shows they were very manoeuvrable and could have attacked the moa with pinpoint efficiency. Some scientists reckon they could have sliced open the poor old moa's backbone to stop them moving.

The moa would drop like a stone and the eagle then flew off to feed its young. Scientists reckon the eagle had to be so big so it could fight off other eagles and fill its belly.

Like the moas, once humans arrived on the islands, the eagles were wiped out straight away. No doubt the eagles thought 'What are those funny looking Moas?' when they saw their first human, and attacked straight away. Sadly for the Haast's eagle, these two legged hairy 'moas' were equipped with deadly stone tools and spears. The poor old eagles were no match for the new arrivals and we will never see their like again.

CHAPTER 9

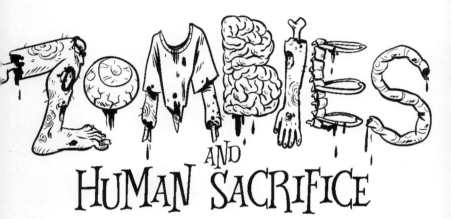

THE DEAD WHO WALK THE EARTH

A long, long time ago in Iron Age Europe (1,200 BCE–50 CE) it is obvious that people believed in zombies. I doubt that they called them zombies, though. The definition of a zombie is 'A dead person who has come back to life.' People in the Iron Age used to sacrifice certain people to their gods and they sure as heck made sure they couldn't come back to life. The dead bodies were stuck in marshes and all kinds of things were put on them to make sure they stayed there.

Here's a story from that time to show you exactly what these zombie-busting pagans got up to.

The young man called Tollund looked over the grassland where he had spent his childhood, raising cattle and sowing barley. Before him was a small forest of myrtle, beech and willow trees. They were all growing next to a swamp where the man's tribe believed the Earth Goddess could be found.

He remembered when he was a young kid and the sun had not shone for many days even though spring had arrived.

Nomrad the wise man knew how to fix the problem. A woman from the tribe who had got up to no good had her head chopped off and was wrapped in a calf skin before she was pushed down into the swamp and covered all over with 'withies' and stones. Withies are strong tree branches that are bent over and each end is pushed firmly into the dirt to pin somebody into the water.

Tolland thought that this was pretty extreme, but as soon as it was done the sun started shining and the crops started growing.

Iron Age sacrifice – choose the odd man out.

But since then things had got worse and Tollund was hungry. Long winters and cool summers had destroyed crops throughout his tribe's lands. He had never had to work the plough or harvest the thin crops as he was the chief's son. But the tribesmen had lost patience. It was time for a sacrifice.

'Just my luck,' thought Tollund. 'I'd prefer to be a scruffy farmer's son rather than the chief's kid any old day of the week.'

At dawn on his last morning, Tolland had a meal of grains and seeds stored from last year's meagre crops and picked from the tribe's lands. Distant cottagers who had not been seen for several years brought grains from this spring's seed crops. Even children provided scraps of meat, which were pounded into the gruel.

'Bugger bugger bum,' thought Tolland as he stood in front of the tribe, stark naked except for a second-hand cape around his shoulders and a hood upon his head. He felt his torc taken from his neck as rope was thrown over his head. The young royal was then forced down until he was on his knees in front of the sacred lake.

'Just my luck to be born into royalty and spend my days hunting, sword fighting and practicing archery, chatting to young maids and riding my chariot. This better bloody work!!!'

That was the last thought that ever entered the young man's head.

A big explosion thumped into the back of his head as Tollund was hit with a wooden club. He was then pushed to the ground as knees crashed upon his back and as he fought for breath another blow on the back of his head knocked him out. Again and again a club bashed in his skull and a rope was tightened around his back so hard that it snapped two vertebrae.

To finish the job his 'loving' tribesmen slit his throat.

All these wounds were inflicted on poor old Tollund so that he could not rise from the swamp.

He didn't feel the cold, still waters cover his corpse. Tollund was placed deep in the swamp and withies were placed over his arms, legs, torso and even his neck to make sure he could not rise and walk like the living dead – like a zombie. Then, just to make sure, a big old stone was put on his back. Why was this done? To make sure he couldn't come back but stayed down with his new BFF: the Earth Goddess.

In fact, for thousands and thousands of years people have taken a lot of precautions to make sure somebody didn't come back from the dead.

How many years to be exact? Possibly 42,000 years.

Now that sure is a long time to believe that zombies have been around. But two different burials in Australia possibly make the connection.

In the Mungo Lake system in central Australia two ancient burials were found. Mungo Man, who was a man, and Mungo Lady, who was a lady.

Both have been dated to around 40,000 years BCE. Back then the whole area was very lush with a lovely big lake packed with fish and turtles and lots of good things to eat. Nowadays it's all desert with only bits of bone and rock sticking out of the surface. That's how Mungo Man and Mungo Lady were found. A scientist saw bits of them sticking out of the sand. Mungo Man was buried very carefully. He was painted in ochre, which is a kind of red mineral, and laid to rest in a pretty comfortable position. He was probably buried with his favourite spear, shield and digging stick, although these have now rotted away.

Not all great archaeological discoveries are planned.

Mungo Lady got an entirely different treatment. She was cremated. Then her bones were broken up. She was then cremated again!! I certainly wouldn't want to be cremated twice that's for sure. She was then buried. Now why, you may ask, was she burnt twice?

157

Did the tribe think she might come back from the dead so it was better just to make sure that they did a very thorough job of it? I don't know the real reason of course, only her tribespeople who also passed away 40,000 years ago really know, but maybe it is an explanation.

ZOMBIE PROOF BURIALS

Now I'm sure you've all been to a graveyard before. Maybe it was to bury Great Uncle Ziggy who always complained about his dicky knee (when he wasn't complaining about 'young people today' and how they should 'get off their backsides dang-nabbit'). Or maybe it was just to walk the dog one windy day in June.

Whatever reason you were there, you no doubt saw lots of headstones. In fact those headstones may be relics of ancient anti-zombie tech. In the Stone Age hunter gatherers would place their dead in a shallow hole (once they had stopped eating them about 200,000 BCE). They would then cover the body with a pile of rocks that we now call a cairn. This cairn had two uses. It stopped wild animals digging up the dead relative and stopped the dead relative rising from the dead. Often a huge boulder would be rolled over the dead body: way heavier than was needed to keep animals out. These stones then evolved into uprights called dolmans (think Stonehenge) and then morphed into the gravestones we see today.

Other early farmers had different ways of making sure their dead didn't come back to bite them on the bum. In Çatal Hüyük in Turkey the folk who lived there in about 8,000 BCE buried their relatives under the lounge room floor! Some houses had up to ten people there. I guess the thinking may have been that if you were living on top of them you could hear it if they wanted to get up to some kind of mischief.

I've seen a lot of zombie movies in my time and you probably have too. What's the best way to kill a zombie? Why, blow out its brain of course. Well this idea isn't just something dreamed up by a schlocky movie director. People have known this for TEN THOUSAND YEARS! Archaeologists in Syria have found that in 8,000 BCE, before people were buried they had their heads bashed in, cut off and buried well away from the body. It seems that this mainly happened to the dead bodies of young men who had died early. Obviously the locals thought that they still had lots of life essence and could come back and cause problems – like hanging around the 8,000 BCE equivalent of shopping malls.

Ancient peoples loved to keep their ancestors close.

Even the Ancient Greeks took measures to make sure their dead didn't rise from the dead. In some areas they pinned them down with heavy rocks and objects before burying them. In modern language we could call this 'a multi-layered resource-rich anti-zombie utilisation programme.'

Another common form of burial was to place the dead body facing downwards. If it woke up and began to dig it would just dig itself deeper. Spooky!

Zombies aren't known for their intelligence.

The Greeks were particularly sure that certain types of people would rise from the dead as revenants. People who had died from the plague, suicide, murder, drowning or a curse, or if they were born illegitimately, were pretty dangerous. They were all buried with millstones, marble, old jugs and rocks to pin them down in the ground. Yowser!

FASCINATING FACTS
CHINESE ZOMBIES
· ·

You all know the classic zombie tends to lurch around a bit and is a bit of slow mover. They tend to overcome innocent people by sheer weight of numbers and begin drooling whenever they come within 100 metres of 'braaaaiiins'.

Jiangshi powdering 'nose'.

Well the Chinese zombie is much more realistic. Rigor mortis has set in and Chinese zombies can only get around by hopping on two legs. The first thing you know about them is the loud 'thump, thump, thump' sound they make. They are called jiangshi, which can be translated as 'rigid body'. People who have been murdered or have committed suicide are most likely to come back as zombies. They might be a bit stiff but jiangshi sure know what they want. They have greenish white skin and often have bits of rotting skin dropping off. They know that to halt the decomposition process they have to suck the life essence out of their victims like a vampire.

If you get attacked by a jiangshi hold a mirror up to them. They are afraid of their own reflections – with good reason.

FASCINATING FACTS
NORSE ZOMBIES
· · · · · · · · · · · · · · · · · · ·

Watch out for the 'again walker' (also known as a draugr) in Sweden and Norway. That is what they call their zombies. These characters really take the cake for being particularly nasty, scary and unsociable. These were the dead bodies of slain Vikings who were re-animated so that they could continue their killing ways. Even in the depths of winter you could smell these bluish-white skinned critters as they stalked their prey. They had unbelievable strength and could crush a man or even a cow like a fortune cookie. It seems that this is the first historical zombie that could infect others with its bite. To kill the draugr (pronounced drow-grr) it was necessary to dismember it and destroy the head. The draugr then had to be burnt and the ashes tossed into the sea.

The draugr had the power of shape-shifting and could even

leave their graves as a wisp of smoke to invade some poor soul's dreams and drive them crazy.

To prevent these post-mortem shenanigans Viking women would do certain things while preparing the dead bodies for burial. Scissors were placed on their chest, twigs and sticks were hidden in their clothes. Their big toes were tied together and pins were driven into the soles of their feet to make sure they didn't walk again. This also had the benefit of checking that the person really was dead! I'd certainly wake up if somebody stuck sharp needles into my pinkie toe!

Not all zombies are this friendly.

*Which would be better? Coming back from the dead
or marrying the dead?*

I'M GETTING MARRIED ...
TO A CORPSE

The Romanians who live in Romania believed that if you die unmarried you will come back as a strigoi. Strigoi are kind of like vampires, zombies and werewolves all mixed up together. They come back from the dead, can shape-shift and love drinking blood. These greenish creatures of the night are pretty unpleasant.

To make sure their beloved daughter or son couldn't come back from the dead, the parents would find some living person of the same age and hold a quick marriage ceremony. I'm not sure if they had a big party with lots of speeches and all of that kind of stuff, but straight afterwards they would bury the groom or bride. Job done.

In this neck of the woods people would also be pretty scared if a mother and baby die during childbirth. To stop them coming back to life the poor pair had to be buried six feet under, below a crossroads, with a stake through their hearts.

THE ORIGINAL ZOMBIE

As we have read, many people through the ages have tried to stop zombies rising from the dead to cause mayhem, terror and death. In Haiti in the Caribbean, however, they actually tried to bring back the dead. It is from this area that the original term 'zombie' comes from. Slaves from West Africa brought their belief in the 'nzambi', which became the creole (a language that combines French and African words) word zombie.

A writer called W.B. Seabrook spent a whole lot of time hanging around with voodoo preachers and wrote a book about it in 1929. The book was called *The Magic Island*.

He left a vivid description of zombies that went something like this:

It seemed that even though the zombie came from the grave, it was neither a ghost, or a person who had been raised form the dead. The zombie is a soulless human corpse, still dead, but taken from the grave and endowed by sorcery with a magical appearance of life – it is a dead body which is made to walk and act and move as if it is still alive. People who have the power to do this go to a fresh grave, dig up the body before it has time to rot, make it move with spells and charms and then make it a servant or a slave. Sometimes it is to commit a crime but usually to drudge around the farm doing the worst boring tasks. They are beaten like a dumb animal if they slack off.

Zombie house cleaning 101.

Seabrook went on to write that everybody on Haiti was terrified of this fate. I would be too, wouldn't you? If the people were rich, they would make sure that their relatives were buried in big marble mausoleums or with heavy stones placed over their graves. Poorer people couldn't afford that so they buried their dead in the garden just behind the back door. That way the relatives could hear any grave diggers going about their wicked, wicked business.

Another option was to bury the dead relative near a footpath, next to a restaurant or even near a market. These spots were always busy, so grave robbers couldn't reanimate people without being found out. Sometimes the family would mount an armed guard with crossbows and shotguns. They would usually stay there 24–7 for three or four days until they were sure their relatives had begun to rot and go all stinky!

Seabrook told a story that he heard from a man. This story happened in 1918 when the sugar cane crop was huge. It was so big that there was a shortage of labour. One sugar plantation owner found a way around this problem. The manager, Old Man Joseph, raised a troop of zombies.

Joseph turned up one morning leading 'a band of ragged creatures who shuffled along behind him, staring dumbly, like people walking in a daze.' As Joseph lined them up for registration, they 'still stared, vacant eyed like cattle, and made no reply when asked to give their names.' They came in single file down from a mountainous village just glimpsed on the horizon.

Joseph explained to the rest of the workers that the new field hands were from a long way away and didn't understand the local creole language.

He soon set them to work, even though most of the other farmers were pretty sure they were zombies. There were men and women and even some young girls in the group. Joseph made sure that they walked as far away from roads and other people as possible, just in case some person recognised one as a dead relative.

At night they would sit around the camp fire staring at nothing and eating plain potatoes boiled in water. Joseph knew that if they ate meat or salt the zombie charm would break.

They ate it without changing expression and lay down every evening to sleep. Of course they didn't really sleep, they were already dead. They just lay there, looking blankly at the roof of their crude hut.

Day after day they toiled. Occasionally they were whipped if they went too slowly, but this seemed not to trouble them.

Joseph would have had free workers for ever, but he made a mistake. In February the local town had their annual fair. Joseph was determined to go as he had lots of money to spend on gambling and good food. He left his daughter Croyance to look after the zombies. But Croyance was a tender-hearted girl and she thought it a shame that these poor women, men and children shouldn't have any fun. Croyance took some coins and led the troupe to the festival. There they sat without expression, looking straight ahead and ignoring the firecrackers, the dancing and the music. Croyance was determined to give them a treat, so she bought a little pastry for each one, thinking they were only made of sugar and flour. But in the middle were small, tasty pieces of salted fish.

The zombies put the treats in their mouth and mumbled and sucked on them. From the group a low moan arose as they all began to sway back and forth. Soon they began to wail and howl. The salt had woken them from their stupor and they realised they were dead. They also realised they were a long way from home.

The poor wailing zombies looked towards their mountain home and began stumbling along the road, mumbling and roaring all the way. None dared stop them for it was now realised they were the walking dead.

Funfair zombie.

As dusk fell the zombies reached their native village on the slopes of the mountain. The people who lived here were also having a celebration and as the file of zombies approached many villagers realised who they were. Fathers recognised dead daughters. Children recognised their dead parents. Some realised they were zombies who had been raised from the grave, while others thought a miracle had occurred and rushed to their loved ones to see if they had returned to life.

The zombies knew better. They wanted to get back to the cold earth of their graves. They ignored the villagers and stumbled up the hill to the cemetery. There they found a plot and dug themselves into the earth.

Home at last.

Seabrook puts it best:

A woman whose daughter was in the procession of the dead threw herself before the girl's shuffling feet and begged her to stay. But the grave-cold feet of the daughter and the feet of the other dead shuffled over her and onward; as they approached the graveyard they began to shuffle faster and rushed among the graves, and each before his own empty grave began clawing at the stones and earth to enter it again. As their cold hands touched the earth of their own graves they fell and lay there, rotting carrion.

YOWSER!

Now you might think this is all a bit of a tall tale and probably a bit silly. But in fact the Haitians took zombies very seriously and there were even formal laws to stop you zombifying your neighbour!

The criminal code of 1883 states that it is illegal to poison somebody to death. It is also illegal to poison someone so that they look dead but are really alive so they can be dug up after burial and used as a zombie slave!

EVOLUTION OF THE ZOMBIE

Now as you know from reading this book, humans have been evolving for millions of years. Well zombies have evolved in less than one hundred years.

The first zombies appeared in movies in the 1930s. They were often African in appearance, had big bulging googly eyes and walked around like sleepwalkers.

The next 'evolution' happened in 1968 with the film *Night of the Living Dead*. Here we saw the next big change, which showed zombies as decomposing, flesh-eating ghouls. They were covered with bite marks, had rotting green flesh and loved the taste of human brains. One bite could infect a person and make them into a zombie. They still walked fairly slowly, but since there were thousands and thousands of them they could be pretty dangerous.

In 2002 the zombie became fully evolved. The movie *28 Days Later* saw zombies as infected with a rage virus. This turned them into red eyed carnivorous freaks that saw a target and ran at it at 100 miles per hour. Every zombie was in fact like an Olympic athlete – very fast and very dangerous.

The BIG QUESTION that you all want to know the answer to is: ARE ZOMBIES REAL? Probably not.

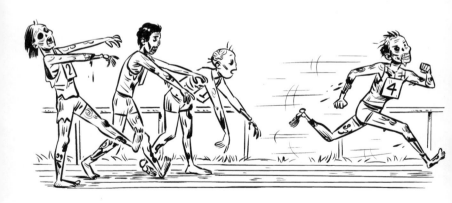

Zombies got a lot faster in 2002!

THE END

We hope you've enjoyed the rip roaring ride through *Monsters and the Supernatural*.

'What?' you say. 'It's finished???'

You may ask, why haven't we talked about the Cyclops, Ghouls, Goblins and Faeries, Demons and Dark Lords? Where are the Golem and the Kraken? Cerberus and Sirens? What about the Rakshasa, Basilisk, Changeling and Snallygaster?

Where's the reference to the Revengeful Revenant?

Don't worry – our next book on monsters will cover all of these crawling critters and lots, lots more.

Meet the Authors

JJ 'Malevolent' Moore
loves to hear scary stories – the scarier the better!

KB 'Monstrous' Moon

doesn't often draw puppies, kittens and flower beds.

First published in 2018 by New Holland Publishers
London • Sydney • Auckland

131-151 Great Titchfield Street, London WIW 5BB, United Kingdom
1/66 Gibbes Street, Chatswood, NSW 2067, Australia
5/39 Woodside Ave, Northcote, Auckland 0627, New Zealand

newhollandpublishers.com

Copyright © 2018 New Holland Publishers
Copyright © 2018 in text: Jonathan J. Moore
Copyright © 2018 in images: Kate B. Moon

A record of this book is held at the British Library and the National Library of Australia.

ISBN 9781760790530

Group Managing Director: Fiona Schultz
Publisher: Alan Whiticker
Project Editor: Rebecca Sutherland
Designer: Andrew Davies
Production Director: James Mills-Hicks
Printed in China by Easy Fame (Hong Kong) Limited

10 9 8 7 6 5 4 3 2 1

Keep up with New Holland Publishers on Facebook
facebook.com/NewHollandPublishers

UK £6.99
US $14.99